THE
HONEYMOON
MYSTERY

A NICK AND KATIE ADVENTURE

HARRY F. BUNN

First published in 2024

DISCLAIMER

The Honeymoon Mystery is a work of fiction. The characters, except for Nick and Katie, are fictitious and not based on real people. Any resemblance is purely coincidental.

ISBN 9798336176551

Dedication

To Nick and Katie

Your wedding on October 26, 2024, is just the beginning of a lifetime of fun, love-filled adventures. Many congratulations on your marriage. With very much love

Dad

Table of Contents

HARRY F BUNN

Chapter One

Where is everyone? Asha brushed a speck of lint from her uniform, which bore her name, her title, Gate Agent, and the logo of her airline. The flight was scheduled to leave in half an hour, but only six passengers had turned up at the gate.

She looked out at the Airbus 320. It was white with its blue Pacifico Airlines insignia and was lightly covered in snow. The aircraft was a well-known narrow-bodied plane manufactured by Airbus with a capacity of 180 passengers, but this and its sister craft had been re-fitted dramatically to carry just 90. The light snowstorm was unusual in early November. The precipitation had ceased half an hour before, and the airport manager, having assessed the situation, declared the airport open for arrivals and departures. A de-icing truck stood ready should frost removal from the aircraft's wings be necessary.

Asha looked to her colleague, a short Hispanic man, who returned her gaze. Surprised at the passengers' absence, she turned her hands upward. He shrugged.

Her smartphone rang and looking down; she saw that it was her manager. "Hi, boss."

He spoke gruffly. "Have you seen the news, Asha?"

"No. I am busy boarding the flight."

"Well, I'll bet you don't have more than a handful of passengers to board."

"Er, right. What do you know that I don't?"

"Snow."

"I can see that, Fred, but air traffic says we should be fine. It stopped snowing an hour ago and was just a dusting."

His voice had a Bronx accent as he started to tell her his thoughts. "The roads are a mess, and, as you know, eighty of our passengers today are in a single party. They're from an organization called BioContra. It just went public and made them all crazy rich. The top people in the company have been given a trip to Bali as a 'thank you' for hard work." He continued, "The fare isn't cheap, and the senior executives have booked the ten First Class Suites up front. The others have Business Class seats in back."

"Fred, I know all that." She consulted her computer screen and entered a few commands. "And, yes, those are the passengers who have not checked in yet."

He gave a hoarse cough. "What you don't know is their fleet of limos and buses from Manhattan had a major pile up on the I-678. Ice. There are police, ambulances, and fire trucks. I don't know the details, but I do know they ain't going to make it to Kennedy in the foreseeable future. You'll only have a half dozen passengers for the flight."

"So, are we canceling the flight?"

"Above my pay grade. I kicked it upstairs for a decision and should hear back any minute. Flying with that few passengers is stupid, but you know Mr. Lee." He paused and then said, "Hang on. I have another call. It's the man himself. I'll get back to you."

Asha stood behind the check-in desk and thought about the airline's owner. She had met him once and was impressed. Lee was a Chinese billionaire who had recently acquired the small

Pacifico Airline and leased six new, narrow-bodied Airbus 320 aircraft for its Pacific fleet. The company outfitted each to provide the highest level of luxury, with ten First Class Suites, one on either side of a center aisle, and eighty Business Class seats, two on each side with fully reclining seats. There was no Economy seating. Everything was top-of-the-line—costly and very high-end. The owner cared more about the image than the profitability of his folly.

Asha's phone rang.

"Mr. Lee says we leave on time."

"But…"

"No buts, Asha. Lee ain't prepared to lose face by canceling one of his first scheduled flights on his most prestigious route."

She sighed and started to activate her microphone, which accessed the public address system to announce boarding. Then, she realized that this was unnecessary. She and Juan could talk to each of the six passengers and board them individually. She called the flight captain, who was already in the cockpit and filled him in. He requested that she come to the cockpit and discuss the arrangements. When there, she made a suggestion. "Only eight will now be flying, and they all have Business Class tickets. Six are here but we're absent the other two. Let's put them all up front, Captain."

"Sounds like a plan."

She returned to the check-in desk, edited the flight manifest, and printed out new boarding passes with the updated First Class seating assignments. She accessed her terminal and verified that the two missing passengers had checked in their luggage, so she also prepared passes for them. Looking out to the assembled six, she thought, *who is who? Let me guess. Having nothing other than the names of the passengers will make it challenging to get it right.* There were two women, and their names were "Teresa Holmes" and "Patricia Feltham." One was young and the other older. Their first names did not indicate age, so there would be a 50:50 chance of guessing correctly. They were standing close to one another but not talking, so she approached and called out the first name, "Ms. Teresa Holmes?" The older woman turned and acknowledged that she was that person. *The other one must be Patricia Feltham.*

Now, what about the men? There were four of them, so this was going to be more challenging. It would be a guess. Each passenger was wearing an overcoat, which they had grabbed as the snow started to fall and the trip to JFK loomed.

She took in the four. One was middle-aged, tall, and rugged. Another was in his mid-thirties, and his expensive overcoat indicated that he was affluent. A third was unattractive and thin, with a professorial look and a serious disposition. The fourth was nondescript. He was medium height, medium weight, and dressed in an old ski jacket. *I give up.*

She asked the six to gather around her and explained the situation, including the accident, and that the BioContra party would not be traveling with them. She informed them of their new, upgraded seat assignments.

Asha was surprised at the reactions of two of the passengers. One, the mid-thirties woman she now knew to be Patricia Feltham, seemed upset. The man dressed in the expensive overcoat also appeared annoyed by Asha's announcement. *Why would they be pissed about being upgraded? Or are they upset about the BioContra people missing the flight?*

Teresa Holmes was suspicious. "Why are you doing this? Why have these other people canceled? With all this snow, are we safe?"

Asha gave her an exaggerated laugh. "Believe me, Ms. Holmes, Captain Reynolds is a very experienced pilot, and he will not put passengers' lives at risk. Not to mention his own. He wouldn't leave the gate if there were any possible danger."

The unattractive, thin man stepped forward. "So, we are all in First Class now. Will we be served First Class meals? First Class drinks?"

"Yes." She took a chance. "Mr. Grange?"

"That's *Doctor* Grange."

Asha looked up from the boarding passes she held. "I'm sorry. *Doctor* Grange. Pacifico prides itself on its service in both cabins, but since you are being upgraded, you'll enjoy an even better experience." She now addressed all six passengers. "Each of you will have what we call a Suite. This is more than just a seat. The Suites are about fifty square feet. I could describe them, but we should do so when you're on board. The flight attendants will show you the ins and outs."

Over the next several minutes, the passengers were escorted onto the aircraft.

Back at the gate, Asha frowned. The A320 would push back in the next few minutes, but the two remaining passengers had yet to show up. She accessed her system and verified that the pair had checked in their luggage. *Where are you two?*

Then she saw a late twenties man and woman, each trailing a carry-on, running down the jetway. They were out of breath and waved passports and boarding passes.

The man called to her. "We're Mr. and Mrs. Bunn. Did we make it?" He looked around at the empty departure area. "Sorry, we're late." He added, "I'm Nick, and this is my wife, Katie."

Asha gave the two new passengers a grin. "You're lucky. We were just about to close the doors."

Katie took the lead, "The traffic was awful. The snow was just enough to slow everything down, and our Uber driver wasn't the best." Nick, who had worked part-time for Uber while in college, nodded his agreement.

The Gate Agent smiled. "Let me just check your passports. You said Mr. and Mrs. Bunn, but your passport and boarding pass, madam, says your name is Pittlekow."

"Yes. That's my maiden name. We were just married and didn't have time to change it. We're on our honeymoon."

"Congratulations. I'll alter the onboard manifest. From now on, you're Bunn."

Asha handed them the new boarding passes she had printed. "Well, I have some good news. There was an accident, and most of the passengers didn't make it. We have just eight, including you two, for the trip. So, we've upgraded everyone to First Class. Everyone has a Suite with both window and aisle access."

Nick and Katie smiled at her, and she shook her head. "You look exhausted, so let's get you on board and settled."

The wedding had taken place on a lake outside Austin, Texas, and it had been a lot of fun but a lot of work. As well, Katie had a demanding job and had suffered health-wise over the past two years. Now, she was married to the man she loved and on her way to their honeymoon in the Pacific Ocean where the two of them could relax, lay in the sun, and swim in the turquoise-blue sea as well as try the latest water sports and explore the hills of these romantic islands. The thought of the upgrade with its larger space for their long flight made her heart sing.

Asha escorted them to the plane, where a flight attendant met them. "Welcome on board, Mr. and Mrs. Bunn. You are in 2A and 2B. My name's Marcia."

As they passed row 1, Nick saw an older lady holding an oversized carry-on. She opened the overhead locker and lifted the heavy case into it. He stepped forward. "Can I help you with that?"

She smiled at him. "So nice. Thanks, but it's fine." She lifted it easily into place, and Nick raised his eyebrows involuntarily.

They reached row 2, and Nick helped Katie place her carry-on in the overhead.

Marcia joined then, asking, "May I get you a drink before take-off?"

Katie answered, "Just a water, please,"

Nick opened the half door leading to 2B opposite and, turning to the flight attendant, said, "What are your specialty cocktails?"

"Our most popular drink is the Manhattan, and our bartender, Ken, has received countless accolades for his version of that classic."

Nick looked at his smartwatch. "It's 5:00 PM. Perfect. a Manhattan sounds great. Thanks, Marcia."

Katie looked around her, taking in the six other passengers. They were removing their overcoats, which the flight attendants stowed in the overhead lockers. Each passenger looked around and marveled at the space and luxury before settling into their seats.

Katie explored her Suite. It had a half door, a large, well-padded seat that she knew would be converted to a fully flat bed when needed, and on the wall facing the seat was a 32-inch television monitor. There was an abundance of various-sized compartments that probably held the bedding and provided storage space for the personal items the passenger chose to access on the flight. There was also a "guest seat". She pointed to it. "Thank goodness. We can visit one another. I was worried that we would each be imprisoned in our separate little luxury cells for the twenty-five hours of the flight."

Marcia brought them their drinks, and they heard a click as the onboard audio system indicated an imminent announcement.

"Good evening, ladies and gentlemen. My name is Jeff Stokes, and I am the Passenger Service Manager for this flight from New York's Kennedy Airport to Denpasar in Bali, Indonesia, with a refueling stop in Los Angeles. Marcia Krebs and Ken Grobe will accompany me in serving you this evening and throughout the flight. Normally, we would have three more flight attendants, but they were caught in the snow, and, with the small number of passengers, we are permitted by the FAA to use this level of staffing. Trust me, your comfort and safety are our prime directive, and we'll take the best care of you." Stokes continued, "Before take-off, we'll be coming through the aircraft to explain how the various aspects of the Suites operate. In the meantime, may I introduce John Reynolds, our captain for the first leg of our flight tonight?"

"This is the captain speaking." Reynolds had a Southern drawl and introduced himself. He provided more details of their flight, including that the A320 they would be flying had been modified with additional fuel storage to allow the nineteen-hour flight from Los Angeles to Denpasar. He added, "Flight time to LAX is five hours and twenty minutes, and our overall journey time is twenty-five hours. My First Officer, Sonia Gonzales, and I will have the pleasure of flying y'all about half of that. For the second half of the flight, you'll have a different crew joining us in LA."

The Passenger Service Manager then called for the passengers to fasten their seatbelts and directed them to the safety video.

A few minutes later, the A320 pulled back from the gate, and Katie looked out of her window as the aircraft tug moved the plane into its position for taxiing. It disconnected from the A320, and Captain Reynolds took control and started to trundle the aircraft forward. He followed the pattern of lights, directing his movement toward the aircraft line waiting to take off. A whirring sound indicated that the flaps had been extended for takeoff, and the new bride settled back in her seat. She glanced over to Nick, who was looking out of his window as the A320 gathered speed.

Ten minutes later, they were airborne en route to Los Angeles, and Katie heard the wheels retracting and the bay door closing over them. Their adventure was starting.

When they reached cruising altitude, the captain turned off the fasten seatbelts sign, and Katie rose and walked over to Nick's Suite. "How's the Manhattan?"

Nick gestured out his window at the city far below them. "It's still there."

"Very funny. I mean your drink."

He raised the empty glass and looked up. "It was great."

Marcia appeared and said, "We have clear skies ahead, so you can make your way to the bar if you wish. The bar has ten stools so that we can

accommodate all our passengers simultaneously."
He chuckled. "No waiting on line."

Nick laughed, "Sounds like a party."

Chapter Two

Nick and Katie were social people who thrived in mixed company. However, they were tired and debated whether to visit the bar and meet the other passengers or enjoy the solitude of their Suites.

Katie raised an issue. "Do you remember that guy we met on that flight to St Louis last year?"

"The taxidermist – who rattled on and on about the fine points of his art? For an hour."

"That's the one. Let's hope there's no one like him on this flight. It was bad enough on that short trip, but it would be unbearable for twenty-five hours."

"At least we can sneak back to our Suites."

Nick pointed to the empty Suites around them. "Looks like everyone's gone to the bar."

Katie leaned over the aisle. "Shall we chance it?"

"Let's. And I have an idea."

She gave a little groan. "What's your idea?"

"While we are on this long flight, I will invent a game we can play to while away the many hours."

"Okay. Tell me more."

"We'll make it up as we go. It's a sort of 'whodunit.' We have six passengers bound together in isolation for a twenty-plus-hour flight—a perfect plot for an Agatha Christie mystery."

Initially skeptical, Katie warmed to the concept. "How would it work?"

"We'll observe each of the passengers and decide who is the likely victim and then try to figure out the likely murderer."

"Sounds like fun." She looked about her. "But we don't even know their names yet."

"True. So, let's join our fellow passengers for a drink and learn about them."

"Let me get organized first." She picked up her backpack and took out the various items she wanted to access during the flight. She stowed each in the separate small compartments and made a mental check to ensure she knew where everything was. "Oh, and if we are going to do it right, we need to include the crew for the game. I count three flight attendants and two pilots in the cockpit. Let's hope the victim is not one of the pilots."

The other six had taken seats at the bar, and Ken was mixing various drinks. Nick whispered, "Take note of what cocktails they order. It's a personality giveaway."

The barman turned to the older, thin woman who had been the last to arrive before Nick and Katie. "What can I get you, madame?"

"Vodka Martini, up with a twist."

"What brand do you prefer?"

"I have no idea. I've never had to decide before. You choose Ken."

Nick sat down, ordered drinks for him and Katie, and opened the conversation. "Hello, I'm Nick Bunn, and this is my new bride, Katie." He then added a little about them: their jobs, where they lived, and their sports and hobbies. He purposely included this descriptive material, hoping it would encourage others to do the same. He held his smartphone and quietly triggered his voice recorder app.

A tall, stocky man dressed in jeans and a yellow Hawaiian shirt extended his hand. He turned to face the assembled passengers, as Nick had done. "Hi everyone. I'm Jim Borders." The man did not elaborate, but Nick and Katie both summed him up in their minds as strong, tanned, and with course hands. He probably has a physical job *outdoors.*

Another at the bar said, "My name is Ned Blackman." Dressed in clothes reflecting the recent snowstorm, the man did not seem keen to make eye contact with anyone else. He, too, offered no further information.

"Marcel Grange. Doctor Marcel Grange." Borders and Blackman each smiled as they introduced themselves. Grange did not. He held a serious expression on his face, and it was obvious that Borders took this as a rebuttal.

A young woman, probably in her mid-thirties, looked away, but Jim Borders prompted her. "What's your name, darling?"

She was drinking water and looked at him with a look that showed she hated him from this first encounter. "Trisha Feltham." Katie was surprised to see that she wore gym clothes.

Borders picked up on this. "You look like you just came from working out."

She hissed at him, "None of your business." But then she appeared to think she needed to explain. "I bought a ten pass and, going away on vacation, wanted to get my money's worth. You're right. I came directly from the gym to Kennedy. Satisfied?"

He followed up. "You're weird. Even when we were told of the BioContra party cancellation and that we would all be upgraded, you were annoyed."

She took a gulp of water and then added, "I'm tired. I'm going to my Suite."

Katie prided herself on detecting when people were lying and was sure there was more to Feltham's story.

While most passengers were dressed casually, one wore a dark, formal suit and tie over a white, starched shirt. His attire matched a New York boardroom, not a flight to a tourist resort on the other side of the world. Borders prompted him. "And you are?"

The man was annoyed and stated coldly, "Anthony Stamford."

"You're dressed up for the flight?"

"I came straight from the office." He returned to sipping the single malt Scotch that Ken had poured him. Borders snarled at him.

The older woman spoke next. "I'm Teresa Holmes. I've lived in Manhattan all my life, but now I'm on the way to Bali. This is my first trip to Asia, and I'm looking forward to an adventure." She seemed excited and had an infectious grin on her face.

The Passenger Service Manager formally introduced himself and the two others on his staff.

A half-hour later, Katie and Nick returned to her Suite, and she reached for her laptop. "I'll set up a spreadsheet and enter the names, and then let's discuss each. I've set it to synch with your laptop, so we'll both have the same, up-to-date sheet."

In addition to the audio recording, Nick had taken notes on his phone and, consulting them, said, "Let's start with the crew. The Passenger Service Manager is Jeff Stokes. The other flight attendants are Marcia Krebs and our illustrious bartender, Ken Grobe."

Katie structured the spreadsheet and entered the names. "By the way, Ken made me a fantastic Keto mocktail. It would be very unfair if he's the murderer."

Nick looked up from his phone. "Worse still, if he's the victim," he continued. "The pilot is John Reynolds, and the First Officer is Sonia Gonzales. They're adding additional crew in LA, so we'll find out their names and add them then."

Katie keyed in the information and nodded for her husband to continue. She reflected on being newly married and smiled. She was still not used to their new, formal, union.

Nick scrolled on his phone and said, "The older lady, Teresa Holmes. My guess is she's a divorcee, but why would she be going to Bali at this time in her life? It's a mystery to me."

"Darling, that's ageist. Just because someone is old doesn't mean they can't go out and have a good time. Take your dad for example."

Nick nodded his agreement. "The young woman, Trisha Feltham, is weird. I'll bet she's a techie."

Katie entered the details as Nick rattled off the other names and his first impressions. Marcel Grange—a doctor of some kind. Anthony Stamford—Wall Street? Jim Borders—an outdoors type. "One interesting point is that although Bali is very much a tourist destination, none of our fellow passengers is traveling with a partner."

Nick looked at the next name she had recorded. "Ned Blackman. He ordered vintage champagne, but we both saw it seemed like a new experience for him. He was surprised it was served in a small glass and swilled it back like a beer."

"And just before everyone left the bar, Borders pushed him to tell us what he did for a living."

"Right. And do you remember his answer?"

"How could I forget? He said he was a homicide detective with NYPD."

As she entered this into the spreadsheet, Katie chuckled, "Well we know now who'll solve our fictitious crime."

Chapter Three

Katie liked the size and comfort of her accommodation but sighed and called to Nick on the other side of the aisle. "I love the Suite, but you are so far away. I wish you were closer, darling."

Nick rose, crossed the passageway, and kissed her. "We'll have lots of time in Bali, but the luxury of this flight is cool. It beats back of the bus Spirit." He continued. "Katie, you look exhausted. The flight to LAX is over five hours long, and we're only an hour into it. Why don't you take a nap? It'll be 8:00 PM local time when we land for refueling."

"Great idea. Now, how do I convert this seat?"

Nick signaled to a flight attendant who walked briskly over to him. "Hi Marcia, can you help Katie get the bed set up."

"Pleased to assist. We're about to serve dinner. Do you want to wait until you've eaten or skip the meal?"

"I'll skip the meal."

Marcia looked at a list she held. "You have a Keto diet. Is that right?"

"Yes."

"If you change your mind about eating now or are hungry later, I'll be able to get you something. We have a bunch of snacks as well."

"We had lunch, so I'll probably not need anything for hours."

Marcia laughed, and Nick liked her a lot. Too often, recently, he had encountered flight attendants who seemed to hate their jobs and loathed dealing with passengers, even the pleasant ones.

The flight attendant reached past Katie into a small cupboard and withdrew a plastic-wrapped package. "Pajamas, if you want to use them. Particularly when we leave LA and head for Bali, most passengers prefer it to their street clothes. During refueling, our airline rules require that everyone disembarks, so you may want to wait till we depart LAX before changing." Katie nodded in agreement, and Marcia returned the blue cotton pajamas to their locker.

Katie said, "I'm going to the bathroom to freshen up."

Five minutes later, she returned to her Suite and saw that Marcia had finished setting up. The flight attendant puffed up a pillow and laid it at the head of what was now a 6ft 6in long and comfortably wide bed. "I'll wake you before we land. Okay?"

Katie was about to settle in when the man who had introduced himself as Jim Borders called out to Marcia. "Just another little drink before dinner."

Nick enjoyed a lobster salad, grilled Wagyu steak, and lemon cheesecake. Ken came around with a choice of wines, displaying his sommelier skills, and Nick accepted his recommendations for the pairings. He used his smartphone to take pictures of each course as it was served and then used the onboard satellite connection to text these to his parents, his brother, James, and James' wife, Rebecca. This was a family tradition.

He considered attempting to doze or, perhaps, sleep, but the adrenalin from the wedding and the ride to the airport through the snow had him wired up. Glancing over at Katie, he saw she was sound asleep and looking as beautiful as ever.

He withdrew his laptop and logged on to the plane's Wi-Fi network and its satellite links to the Internet. He then downloaded the spreadsheet that Katie had constructed and stored in the cloud. His mind explored further optional information that would add to their game and included a few additional columns for data. His entrepreneurial brain turned to the concept of an AI-based app that would…

Nick used the fast internet channel to Google "Murder Mystery App" and, for the next half hour, checked out the various whodunit games that were available. There were a lot but perhaps he could include something that would be differentiating and unique. His friends, Nathan and Ali, would help.

He looked down at the screen of his laptop. *I have the structure, but I need to validate it.*

Sitting in seat 1A, Jim Borders rose and passed Nick, returning to the bar again. *Why not use the outdoorsy guy as a test case?*

Nick watched as the man approached Ken, who stood behind the bar polishing a glass. He sat next to Borders and noticed the NYPD detective opposite him nursing another glass of champagne and still looking out of place with this choice of beverage. Borders, in a firm voice, called over to the NYPD cop. "What've you got there? Champagne?"

"Yes. It's French."

"It has to be French, or they can't call it Champagne."

"Really?" Blackman frowned at this newfound knowledge.

Borders gestured to the barman. "Ken, what do you have in the way of cognac?"

The barman pointed to the bottles in front of him. "I have an excellent, Courvoisier XO."

The passenger nodded. "Sounds good."

Nick glanced at Borders and spoke. "Enjoyable meal?"

The man raised his eyes from his glass. "Yes. It was. I had high expectations, but it surpassed them."

"What did you order?"

"The Wagyu beef."

"Me too."

Ken turned his attention to Nick and asked, "Drink, sir? What can I get you?"

"A bourbon."

"I have Stagg or Old Carter."

"Stagg, please."

Nick smiled at the man beside him at the bar. "I think you said your name was Jim Borders when we introduced ourselves."

"That's right."

"What do you do?" Nick hoped that his directness would not offend the man, but it did.

Borders bristled, but his cognac seemed to calm him down a bit. "I have a construction company," he said.

"Commercial?"

"No. Residential. I specialize in roofs. Tile, shingle, steel. You name it, we do it."

Nick followed up. "You must be making a fortune in the current housing boom." He left the statement dangling.

Borders appeared comfortable talking about his business. "Right on. About half my work is new construction, but, particularly in New York just now, thousands of older homes need replacement roofs. That's where I make most of my money, except in the winter. That's when the damage often becomes apparent, but we can't replace the roof in subzero temperatures. We patch it, sign a contract, and wait until spring before we start."

Nick asked, "So, are you off to Bali for a roofing project?"

"No. Strictly pleasure." He paused and sipped his cognac. "I'm sick of the snow in New York state, and we have little to do except interim repair work in the winter. I'm off to lay on a beach and soak up the sun. Californians say that snow is something you drive *to*, not *in*. That's my view as well."

"You're traveling alone?" Nick tasted the bourbon, which was excellent.

Borders hesitated and looked away. "Yes. My wife doesn't like hot weather, so she stays home to look after the dogs. She'll be happy to have me out of the house. In most winters, we're stuck together too long. A marriage needs space." He brought the brandy balloon to his lips and savored the taste of the Courvoisier. "You said you and your lovely wife just got hitched. Congratulations."

"That's right. Just a week ago." Nick's mind switched from the mystery game he was working on to the wedding Katie and he had just experienced.

The pair had chosen the Retreat at Balcones Springs in Marble Falls, an hour north of Austin, Texas. Katie's family came from all over the U.S. and even Guam in the Pacific. Nick's considerably smaller family lived in Connecticut and St. Croix, and the newlyweds' friends were mainly from New York.

The ceremony took place in a church on the lake, and the reception followed at the Retreat. The night before, a party was staged "cowboy" style' on a nearby ranch.

Borders raised an eyebrow to catch Ken's attention and tapped the side of his empty glass. The barman reached over and topped him up. "Thanks, Ken." His words were becoming slurred.

Nick did not count drinks but knew Jim Borders had consumed at least five and probably more over the evening meal. He thought *a man who borders on being drunk*, smiling at his pun. If this man were to be the murderer, he was not acting like someone who needed his wits about him when committing the crime. Perhaps he could be struck off the list of suspects early in the plot. Or maybe he would be the victim. Or was he putting on a show or an act and was brighter than he appeared?

The A320 landed at Los Angeles International Airport on time and taxied to its designated gate.

"Hello again. This here is the captain. We've arrived at LAX, and I'd like to welcome you. As I mentioned earlier, this stop is to refuel for the next leg of our flight, but we require passengers to exit the aircraft during that operation. Refueling only takes about twelve minutes, but I'm looking at a thirty-minute process by the time the tanker truck is in position and hooked up. Pacifico has a lounge at the gate with drinks and some fresh snacks. See y'all back here shortly."

The announcement paused, but then the captain continued, "Our onward flight will be about nineteen hours, so we have a relief cockpit crew joining us here. My First Officer and I will fly you for the next five hours, and then the new guys will take over while we get some good ole' shut eye. Captain Anton Silofski heads up the new crew. He's a Ruskie."

Nick and Katie left the plane with the other passengers and cabin staff. Nick looked around and said, "Let's use the time to check out one or more of our characters."

Katie was warming to the evolving game. "The NYPD detective has to be a key player, so let's start with him."

They found Ned Blackman chewing on a plate of steamed shrimp. Nick took out his smartphone and made a few notes about the man's appearance—medium height, medium weight, and a forgettable face. He was wearing jeans and an open-necked long-sleeve shirt. Nick noted that his clothes were inexpensive and old for someone on a detective's salary. They did not match his purchase of a Business Class ticket to Bali. *Maybe he doesn't care about what he wears*, Nick thought.

He called out. "Hi, Ned."

Between mouthfuls, Ned Blackman answered them. "Hi."

Katie took the lead. "Wow. You're a detective. That must be a tough job." She hoped Blackman would pick up the conversation.

He put the plate down and reached for a glass filled with champagne. He gulped it down and said, "Yes." He poured himself another.

This is going to be hard work, Nick thought.

However, the man continued, "New York is a rough city. We have some of the worst scumbags in the world, and it takes a lot to get the better of them."

Katie sprang on his words. "You must be one smart dude. Which precinct are you in?"

He hesitated before answering. "Fifteenth."

"Oh, on Elizabeth?"

"Yes. That's the place."

The tall, thin man they knew to be Dr. Marcel Grange joined them. He did not smile. "The newlyweds, isn't it?" He ignored Blackman.

Katie smiled. "Yes. Nick and Katie."

He took a chilled bottle of water from the ice bucket in front of them and, uncapping it, took a swig. "Staying hydrated is important, particularly on these long flights."

After some small talk about the flight, Nick said, "Marcel Grange. Marcel's a French name."

"My mother was a Parisian. My father was British."

Katie said, "Do you have a practice in the U.S.?"

He let out a hollow laugh. "I don't have a private practice and never have had one. I started as a toxicologist working in the hospital system but became fed up with the bureaucracy, the long hours, and the low pay. It cost me my first wife."

He became silent, and Nick, who had noticed that the bottle of water he had been drinking was empty, said, "More water?"

"Yes. Thanks"

Nick reached over and handed him a fresh bottle.

Katie picked up the conversation. "So, did you switch professions?"

The toxicologist let out another dry laugh. "No. I joined a biotech company. I use my medical training in a research job. Reasonable hours and a huge pay increase." He sipped the water.

Something occurred to Nick. He remembered a discussion at the bar over introductions. "The biotech company. Is it the same one that had the huge party booked on this flight?"

"No. We're a major competitor."

"What do you do there?"

"I research poisons and work in a team, developing antidotes."

Katie thought of the game and turned to Nick. "Perfect."

Marcel Grange looked at her questioningly, but before he could ask about her comment, Jeff Stokes tapped a fork against a glass to gain the passengers' attention.

"Refueling is now complete. May I request you reboard the aircraft?"

The eight of them finished their food and drank their drinks before making their way to the plane.

Katie motioned towards the woman in her mid-twenties who had looked out of place from the beginning. Her clothes were undoubtedly more suited to a gymnasium or spa than an air flight to a tropical vacation island. Calf-length pants of tight

Lycra and a matching top, both in bright hues of purple. Katie remembered her from when each of the passengers had introduced themselves. "Tricia Feltham." But she noticed something else and mentioned it to Nick. "She seems paranoid about her laptop and her backpack. I can understand not wanting to leave them on the plane but look at how she clutches them to her body. And she keeps looking around her." She gave Nick a wink. "Perhaps she has something on her hard drive that she wants to protect at all costs. Secret plans? We could make her a spy."

As they boarded, Trisha Feltham looked side to side and then approached Katie. "Can I trust you?"

Katie was surprised by the question. "Most people do."

Feltham again looked about her as if expecting an enemy to appear. "I think I'm in danger. People want me dead. Can you help me?" Her eyes were wide and displayed what Nick took to be a severe mental issue. He stepped forward to support his new wife. "Hey. Nobody can hurt you. You're on a plane with a half dozen passengers, and we've all been screened by TSA. No one could smuggle a weapon on board. You're as safe here as you will ever be."

Trisha Feltham's mouth opened to speak, and then she seemed to change her mind but said, "Never mind." She walked quickly to her Suite, entered it, and closed the half door.

Katie turned to Nick. "I hope she's alright."

"Nutcase."

Chapter Four

As they took their seats, a new voice broke through the quiet of the forward cabin. "Hi, folks. My name is Anton Sirofski, and I am joining to relieve Captain Reynolds. He will be flying you for next five hours, and then my First Officer and I take over for the remainder of the flight."

Katie yawned and spoke across the aisle. "Sirofski has a distinctly Russian accent. He's a great character for the game. He could be in league with the gymnast, Ms. Feltham."

Nick grunted his agreement.

Katie rose from her Suite and walked over to Nick. She whispered. "We need to keep a close eye on our detective friend."

"Really? You don't want to cast him as the cop who solves the mystery?"

"There's something wrong with him. He said he's a member of the 15th precinct."

"Yes. On Elizabeth."

"The 15th is on West 10th. It's the 16th that's on Elizabeth."

Captain Reynolds' voice came from the plane's speaker system. "It's late, folks, so I'm going to have the flight attendants dim the cabin lights and let you catch some sleep. If you wish to change into your pajamas, now is a good time to do it. Now, don't y'all be shy."

Most of the passengers, including Katie, withdrew the pajama sets and made for the bathrooms to change before settling down for the night.

Nick commented, "Nice sleepwear. But in the gloom, everyone looks the same. Make sure you come back to the right Suite."

When she returned, Nick leaned across the aisle. "Are you going to sleep?"

Katie shook her head. "No. I slept most of the way to LA and now feel wide awake. You?"

"I dozed a little."

She accessed the online guide. "I think I'll watch a movie."

Nick was still fixated on the murder mystery game he was developing. He said, "I'm going to add more notes on the characters. The stop in LAX gave me some new pieces to add to the puzzle."

'Want some help?"

"Not just now. Let me make my notes, and we can discuss it later."

Katie tuned in to a new release movie, and Nick drew a seating plan based on the various characters identified.

Row 1 – Jim Borders – Teresa Holmes

Row 2 - Katie - Nick

Row 3 – Anthony Stamford – Trisha Feltham

Row 4 – Marcel Grange – Ned Blackman

So, he thought, w*hat do I know about the players so far?*

He followed the seating plan and started with Jim Borders. *He's a pretty straightforward guy. He's a roofing contractor in Upstate New York. He seems successful, but he drinks too much.*

Opposite the roofer was Teresa Holmes. *She is a New Yorker, and I guess she is unmarried. Bali is an odd vacation choice compared to Florida or the Caribbean. She is physically strong for someone of her age and frame.* Nick had watched her easily lift her heavy carry-on into the overhead compartment.

He and Katie were in Row 2.

Anthony Stamford and Trisha Feltham occupied the Suites in Row 3. *Stamford was evasive, wearing costly clothes and shoes. He was arrogant. I don't know what he does for a living, but it pays well. Feltham is probably a techie. Programmer? Is she really scared for her life? She treasures her laptop. It's a weird outfit to be traveling in. Did she really come directly from a gym?*

The fourth row completed the passenger list. *Suite 4A is Marcel Grange. Toxicologist. Works for a competitor to BioContra. Suite 4B is Ned Blackman. Our, maybe, New York City cop. Interesting error that Katie picked up. Is he a fraudster?*

Nick nodded his satisfaction at what he had so far. There were gaps, but he had an initial take on each player. *Whodunits thrive on linkages between the suspects. Are there any here? Doctor Grange has a tenuous link to BioContra and openly identified them as a serious rival, but there are no other apparent connections.*

A voice from the seat behind him interrupted his thoughts. It was the techie, and she called to Marcia: "I have to send an email urgently. How do I get onto the Wi-Fi system?" The flight attendant helped her gain access and offered to help her set up the bed.

"It's okay. I'll do that myself."

A minute or two later, Nick heard a rapid staccato of keystrokes as Feltham addressed whatever urgent need she had. He heard her shift the seat to its bed position. However, a few minutes after that, as he started to doze, he became aware of a scuffling sound behind him that lasted a minute or two. Then, the cabin reverted to silence, only interrupted by the vibration of the plane's engines and faint snores from one or two passengers.

Out of half-asleep eyes, Nick looked over at his new wife, and a broad grin took over his face. She was engrossed in the movie, and he closed his laptop, stowed it in a cabinet, and pressed his call button. Marcia appeared almost immediately.

He was surprised. "Don't you ever sleep?"

She laughed. "I caught a few hours after we left Kennedy, and it's my turn back on again."

Nick rose from his seat. "I noticed you added another cabin crew member in LA."

"Yes, that's right. Sharon Brown. Lovely girl. Anyway, what can I get you?"

"Can you help me make the bed up?"

Marcia gave a toss of her head. "It's better if I do it myself."

"Okay. I'll head off to the bathroom and change into my super-soft pajamas."

As he left, Nick glanced at the Suite behind him. The techie had not changed, was curled up and not moving. He picked up his pajamas and set off to the front of the plane.

When he returned a few minutes later, his bed was extended and made up. The flight attendant put down his pillow, and Nick yawned. He looked over and saw that Katie had finished her movie and was sleeping peacefully. His Suite was still as he crawled under the light blanket, and within a minute, he was asleep.

Three hours later, as he started to wake up, Katie joined him in his Suite.

"Hi. Darling."

"Good morning."

"With all this time change, I'm unsure whether it's morning or night."

"It's still dark outside."

A man appeared out of the gloom of the plane's dimmed lighting. It was the Passenger Service Manager, Jeff Stokes. "Hi, Nick and Katie. Did you get some sleep?"

Katie replied, "Absolutely. These beds are terrific."

Stokes smiled at the two of them. "Can I get you something? Breakfast? Coffee? Something stronger?"

Nick sighed. "What I need is coffee."

"And you, madam?"

"I'll take coffee too. I'm getting hungry, but I'll wait a bit."

He disappeared to the galley, and Nick pulled his blanket away from the bed and activated the lever, which converted it back to a seat. Katie returned to her Suite and did the same. "Care to visit me, Nick?"

Nick stood, crossed the aisle, and took the "guest" seat in Katie's Suite. "How was the movie?"

"Good. Not excellent but fine for a plane ride. I didn't need to concentrate on the plot or the characters. It just flowed over me."

She paused as Jeff laid a small tray with a cup of steaming coffee, a pitcher of cream, and a container of various sweetening alternatives on a shelf in her Suite. On the side were two cookies.

Katie asked him, "Do you have any nuts? I can't eat cookies."

He nodded, "Of course. You follow a Keto diet. I'll get you some. Macadamia nuts?"

"Great." She turned to Nick. "Did you sleep?"

"Yes. I think I was out for some time." He consulted his smartwatch. "Wow, three hours."

She asked, "What time is it?"

He chuckled. "It's 2 AM Eastern, 11 PM Pacific, and in Bali, it's 1:00 PM tomorrow."

"The International Date Line."

"Yes."

She sipped her coffee and Jeff brought Nick's and a bowl of nuts.

The Passenger Service Manager said, "Just for information purposes, we have just changed pilots. Captain Silofski has taken over for the remainder of the flight."

After Jeff left, Katie turned to Nick. "Did you make any progress on the game?"

"I have a profile for each character, but there are gaps."

"Any connections?"

"Nothing obvious. Perhaps the doctor and BioContra."

Katie looked thoughtful. "Do you think it's a coincidence that all the BioContra people missed the flight?"

Nick laughed. "Our game is fiction, so we can decide that for ourselves. Maybe the murderer wanted more people on board to make the plot harder to untangle. With just our eight, the sleuth has a more manageable task."

Katie ran her fingers through her hair. "You keep saying *murderer*, so your game involves a murder?"

"That's why they call it a murder mystery. It'll be a *cozy mystery*."

"Cozy?"

"The definition of a *cozy mystery* is that there is no violence and no sex."

"Oh." Katie angled her head. "So, have you determined the victim?"

Nick smiled. "It's not going to be you or me." He paused before continuing, "How about this? I don't know much about him yet, but what if Anthony Stamford is in finance and decides to short the BioContra stock after its IPO? The stock price could drop like a stone, and all the investors lose a bunch of money. Would that be enough for someone to kill him?"

Katie was skeptical. "Could be. But how can he pull off the murder? What would he use as a weapon? With the TSA checks, smuggling a lethal weapon on board is impossible. You made that point to Tricia Feltham."

Nick stood up, stretched, and saw that Jeff Stokes and Marcia were serving a light breakfast to those who wanted it. The flight attendants left those still sleeping to enjoy their repose, but most passengers were awake and taking refreshments. Trisha Feltham, however, still appeared to be asleep.

Nick noticed that her laptop was open before her as Marcia reached over and gently shook her. She gave no response. Her head looked towards the window, but the shaking caused her to slump forward, and the flight attendant saw her distorted face. Teresa Felltham's eyes were wide open, staring into space. She was dead.

Chapter Five

Marcia pulled her hands to her face and let out a short cry. But she recovered quickly and whispered to her manager. "I think she's dead, Jeff."

Stokes reached over and checked Trisha Feltham's pulse. "I think you're right, but we need to go through the protocol. Start the CPR, and I'll get the defibrillator." The Passenger Service Manager looked down at the dead woman and added, "Protocol says we keep this quiet, but with all the other passengers being within a row or two, everyone's going to know about this pretty soon."

An idea struck him. "Hey, we have a doctor on board. I'll get him to take a look."

He walked back to the next row and interrupted Marcel Grange, who was finishing his breakfast. "Doctor, we have a medical emergency. Can you look at someone? Just one row forward?"

Grange had observed the actions of the cabin crew and was not surprised by the request. "Sure. I'm pleased to help, but I am not a practicing medic. I was once, but I've been doing research for the past twenty years."

Stokes said quietly, "You're the only one on board with medical training. The flight attendants all have first aid skills, but you know more than we do."

The doctor nodded. "Alright. I'll do what I can."

He rose, crossed the aisle, and, seeing that Marcia was already attempting revival using a standard CPR technique, motioned for her to stop so he could make his assessment. He felt for a pulse, examined her body, and found no evidence of any injury. "I believe that this woman is dead. Probably a heart attack, but I don't have the equipment to verify a cause of death."

Marcia said quietly, "Her face is horrific. It's twisted."

Grange nodded. "That's rigor mortis. It happens quite quickly. This makes the time of death about two or three hours ago. Maybe a little more."

The flight attendant looked away. It was going to be a long time before she would forget Trisha Feltham's dead body lying there. She shuddered.

Jeff Stokes' voice broke the silence. "Are you okay, Marcia?"

"Not really. But I'll cope."

Nick, from Katie's Suite, had a clear view of the proceedings and vaguely remembered the noise he had heard from the seat behind him a few hours before.

Ken Grobe appeared with the aircraft's emergency medical kit, and Dr. Grange selected the stethoscope and used it to verify Trisha Feltham's lack of heartbeat.

He sighed. "Yes. She's dead."

Stokes spoke to the barman. "Ken, inform Captain Silofski. As senior captain on the flight, he's officially in charge."

"Right away."

Grange leaned forward toward the face of the dead woman but pulled his head back. "Strange. Her face smells of almonds."

Marcia shook her head. "It can't be what she ate. We had nothing in her evening meal like that, and we didn't pass out nuts like we used to. We're careful about that with so many people having allergies these days. She certainly didn't request any."

The doctor nodded, "Perhaps the smell is from her makeup or perfume."

Jeff looked down at the body. "No. She's not wearing any, so it must be something else."

Nick and Katie stood back but saw what was taking place. Katie spoke quietly to Nick. "He's right. She doesn't have any makeup on. Weird."

Marcia became aware of the small crowd of passengers assembling behind her and turned to them. "We have a medical emergency here. Please return to your Suites so we have room to address it."

Teresa Holmes took in the scene and asked, "Is she alright?"

Grange looked up at her and said bluntly. "No. She's dead."

Marcia shooed the woman back to her seat.

Nick and Katie had emerged from Katie's Suite but returned to it on Marcia's request.

Katie spoke quietly to Nick. "Interesting. With something like his, normally, everyone is curious, but two people weren't. Ned Blackman and Jim Borders didn't even seem to notice. And Anthony Stamford didn't leave his Suite despite being opposite our deceased passenger. He had a good view of what was going on from there."

Nick could see that Grange had a mystified look on his face. Then, the doctor seemed to notice something. He lowered his head and peered closer at Feltham. "What's that?"

Marcia, who was closest to Grange, seemed to notice his interest in the deceased's face. "Have you found something, doc?"

"Look at her nostril. The left one."

"It's red and distorted."

"Yes, Marcia. It is."

"What's that indicate?"

"I don't know. It's as if something was rammed up her nose."

"Why would she do that?"

"I don't know. It tore the skin inside the nostril so that it would have been painful."

The captain, Anton Sirofski, appeared and asked for a briefing by Jeff and Grange. He stood straight and announced, "I'll call this in. There's nothing gained from returning to LA, so cover up passenger. I will have authorities at Denpasar, meet us on arrival and take over. I'll let Pacifico customer relations know. They should have contact for Ms. Feltham and can inform of her death."

Sirofski turned and returned to the flight deck.

Grange looked back at the deceased passenger. He frowned and spoke, half to himself. "That nostril is a mystery. It would have hurt a lot for Feltham to thrust something up her nose herself. I wonder why she would do that. My guess is that it occurred at her time of death." He looked around the Suite. "Whatever she used, it isn't visible now. See if you can find it, Marcia."

Marcia searched the area but could not locate anything out of place.

The doctor stood back and then reached over to the dead woman's nose. He sniffed and then threw his head back quickly.

"Marcia, please ask Mr. Blackman to join us. And ask the captain to return here as well."

She looked quizzically at him but replied, "Will do." She turned, proceeded back to Row 4, and spoke to the man who described himself as a homicide detective: "Mr. Blackman, or is it Detective Blackman? The doctor would like a word."

Nick strained forward to ensure he heard everything that was transpiring.

Blackman had just finished his breakfast and, aware of an incident in the row in front of him, shrugged.

Unbuckling his seat belt, he rose and stepped out into the aisle.

Grange met him there. "Ned, isn't it?"

"Yes. Ned Blackman."

"I think we might have a problem here."

Blackman looked over to the passenger, who now had a blanket draped over her body. "I'm a detective, not a doctor. Or a mortician."

Captain Sirofski joined them. "Marcia said you wanted speak with me."

Grange indicated the empty bar area behind the rows of passengers. "Let's talk there."

Katie turned to Nick. "Time for me to eavesdrop further."

When the three men reached the bar, Grange stopped and addressed the captain. "You probably don't know, but I'm not a normal doctor. I'm a toxicologist. I deal with poisons and their anecdotes."

Silofski said, "Okay. But what that mean?"

Blackman stared into space.

The doctor continued. "The postmortem symptoms make me believe that we have something other than a natural death. She, or more likely another party, rammed something up her left nostril and it smells of almonds. Classic bitter almonds. My guess is that it was a nose inhaler filled with a cyanide solution. I believe Ms. Feltham may have suicided but since there is no sign of the inhaler, it's more likely she was murdered."

Chapter Six

As the three men spoke, they did not notice Katie at the end of the bar, helping herself to a sparkling water. As she listened, she sighed. Nick's game had ceased being a game.

The captain shook his head. "Come on, Doctor. Murder? That's not right. That sort of thing happens in movies, not real life."

Dr. Grange addressed Sirofski's concern. "I may be wrong, but I've spent most of my career researching poisons, and this has all the signs of one."

Blackman did not speak.

Captain Sirofrki said what was on their minds, "If you're correct, Doctor, the murderer is still on board. Is one of passengers."

Grange added, "Or one of the crew."

The captain's voice was firm and decisive. "Alright. I need to check with base, but we have approximately twelve hours remaining flight time. There's nowhere convenient to land, so it makes sense to fly on to Bali. On landing, I'll let the local police assume control. They will either confirm or refute your diagnosis, doctor." He paused, his gaze shifting to Ned Blackman. "I understand you are NYPD homicide detective. We can start police work immediately. This reassure passengers that they are safe. If doctor is right and this murder, it also ensure that murderer doesn't have chance escape justice. Or commit another killing."

Blackman turned white. "Hey, I'm on vacation. I don't want to be involved."

Grange was astonished by his reaction. "I don't think you have a choice. Surely, it's part of the job you took on when you joined the force."

Ned said, "It's outside my jurisdiction." He lapsed into silence.

Katie quietly returned to her Suite. "Nick, my love, your murder mystery game is no longer a game."

He had been using his laptop and looked up. "What do you mean?"

She filled him in and added, "Sirofski wants to have our NYPD detective run an initial investigation. But, based on what we know about him, I think we may have a problem."

"I agree. It could be that he's the murderer and posing as a detective." Nick peered out and saw the doctor return to his seat. The captain strode past them, heading for the cockpit, and Ned Blackman stood alone in the bar area. He appeared uncertain and a little angry.

Nick said, "Let's go and confront Blackman. See if we can verify our suspicions."

Katie put her hand on Nick's arm. "Is that wise? If he is the killer, he might add us to his target list."

"Perhaps we should just keep our heads down. Stay out of this."

Katie shook her head. "No. I can't do that. Trisha Feltham asked me for help, but I turned her away. Maybe I could have prevented her death."

"Rubbish. We had no idea that she was actually in danger."

Katie continued. "One thing we can do is to try our best to identify her killer. We can't bring her back, but we can see that justice is served."

Nick said, "Okay. Let's start with Mr. Blackman. If he's in charge of the investigation, and he is also the murderer, it could be dangerous for us. Let's hope this is not a very short marriage." He packed away his laptop, and the two of them walked the dozen steps to the bar and saw that Blackman was still there. He was white and shook his head when he noticed them approaching.

"I heard everything," Katie said to the man.

Blackman turned his head from side to side, and it seemed he had made a decision.

"Hi. I guess I'm running the investigation."

She looked him squarely in the eyes. "Perhaps not, Ned. You're not really a detective, are you?" It was a risk, and Nick watched the man closely.

Blackman's complexion became even whiter than it had been earlier. "Why do you say that? Of course, I am."

"You said you are in the 15th precinct in Manhattan, right?"

"Yes."

"And you said you worked on Elisabeth, right?"

"Er, yes."

"Well, you didn't do your homework, Ned. The 15th is not on Elizabeth. That's the 16th precinct."

"Oh, shit."

"Tell me the truth."

He seemed about to cry. "You're right. I'm not a detective. I'm not even a police officer. I work in building security. I sit at a desk in the lobby and sign people in when they come for meetings."

Katie gave a bitter laugh. "So, why did you lie?"

The man looked across the bar as though he needed a drink. Instead, he turned to the newlyweds. "Everyone else on board seems so clever and rich. I've always wanted to be something other than a security guard, but I've never managed to get out of the rut. I've saved for years for a trip like this and needed to be a part of the up-market crowd. Saying that I am a homicide detective seemed so easy."

They heard purposeful steps approaching, and the captain joined them. He regarded Nick and Katie curiously but said to Blackman, "Everything is set up. My management agree my recommendation and have confirmed with Indonesian police. I'm still not fully convinced is murder but you are to secure scene, conduct initial interviews, and search for whatever device used as weapon. You are officially in charge of investigation."

Ned said quietly, "Oh, shit."

Silofski him a quizzical look.

Nick stepped forward. "We're up to speed on the case, and Detective Blackman has asked us to assist him. We'll organize the interviews for him and help out." Katie looked at her husband in disbelief.

The captain appeared suspicious of the arrangement but nodded. "Sounds like plan. I notify my management, and you start investigation."

Katie and Nick returned to her Suite, and she shook her head, "Are you insane, Nick?"

Nick sighed. "I couldn't hang Blackman out to dry." He looked at his smartwatch. "I calculate we have about eleven hours before we land. We may not be able to crack the case, but we're good at interviewing people, and we can easily record their answers. Eleven hours should provide a lot of intel. They say that if a crime can't be cracked in the first 24 hours, it won't be cracked at all."

"They?"

Nick threw up his hands.

Katie looked at her new husband. "I guess you're right. I owe that to Trisha Feltham, and our observations of the players and the notes you made for your game idea give us a great start." She paused before saying, "We need to be clever about this. Ned must take the lead, and then we can ask questions to clarify the answers. It can't appear that we are running the show, although I don't expect much help from our security guard."

Nick stood. "One important thing, though. This is no longer a game. One, or maybe more, of the passengers or crew is a cold-blooded murderer, and if they think we are onto them, we could be in danger."

She smiled at him, "Have you forgotten? I like excitement."

Nick saw Ned Backman approaching them. "Hey, thanks for not ratting me out."

Nick pointed a finger at the man. "You realize it's a crime to impersonate a police officer."

Blackman hung his head, "It was a prank. I just told a bullshit story. I didn't try to con anyone." He paused, looked around, and said, "What do we do next? I'm not a detective, and I don't know anything about investigating. Or even where to start."

Katie said, "Surely, you've read whodunits. You search for clues, interview everyone individually, and look for answers that don't hang together."

He let out a gasp. "Oh God."

Nick followed up. "I meant what I said to the captain. We'll help. Perhaps we'll do most of the work. I've already been taking notes and have a lot of material in a spreadsheet."

Blackman had been hanging his head but now looked up. "What on earth prompted you to do that?"

"It doesn't matter. But let's sit down and go over what I have and any other observations one of us has made. Let's go to the back of the plane, Business Class. It's empty, and we won't be disturbed." He added, "Or overheard."

When they reached an area halfway through the deserted rear of the aircraft, Nick motioned for Blackman to take a seat. "We'll set up here."

Ned Blackman looked around and slumped down. "I don't know I can do this."

Katie looked at him. "Yes, you can, Ned. This is how it'll work. Nick and I'll develop a list of questions for each of our suspects, and you will ask them one by one. When they respond, Nick and I will drill down with additional queries. Everyone must see that you're heading up the investigation, or it won't work."

Blackman's face showed a pained expression, and he said quietly, "Okay. I'll try."

The captain's voice, with his distinctive accent, came across the speaker system. "Ladies and gentlemen. I'm sure you all know that passenger died while on flight. My management has reached out and offered condolences to woman's family. Examination by doctor on board suggests death may not be from natural cause so I have asked Detective Blackman to conduct initial investigation. He'll interview each of you and have report ready for authorities in Bali when we land. Please cooperate with detective." He continued, "We shall not be changing our course and will still head directly to Denpasar. You not be inconvenienced."

Katie turned to Ned. "Well, you said you wanted to be someone you are not, and now you have your wish. You've been appointed chief investigating officer."

He gasped. 'I'm out of my depth. I will be relying on you two to make up for that."

Nick started. "I've drawn up a cabin layout with everyone's Suite shown. Oh, and I think I know the time of death. The lights had been dimmed, and everyone was settling down when I heard a scuffle behind me. I didn't pay any attention to it at the time. It's now nearly 4:00 AM Pacific Time, which would have been about 1:00 PM. The time matches the doctor's comment that the rigor mortis on Trisha Feltham's face would have set in after 2 or 3 hours."

Katie said, "What was the motive? What would have prompted someone to kill her? And having cyanide available implies premeditation. This was not just a random attack. It was planned."

Nick nodded his agreement. "Let's check her belongings."

Blackman asked, "Are we allowed to do that? The woman is dead."

Katie replied. "That's what investigators do."

They proceeded back to the Suite where Feltham's body lay, covered in a blanket. Nick spotted her open laptop computer and smartphone. "The laptop's gone into 'sleep mode,' and we'll need her password to get access." He looked about the Suite. "If she was the techie, we thought she was, that's not going to be *password1* and I'll bet she didn't have it written down where we'll be able to find it."

Katie picked up the laptop. "Her PC has a biometric sensor that would read her fingerprint. There are two main technologies, but each only works when the finger is attached to a living person. We should try it anyway." Katie reached under the blanket and withdrew Feltham's right hand. "She was right-handed, wasn't she?"

Blackman answered, "No. Left-handed."

"Okay." Katie took the first finger of the dead woman's left hand and placed it on the sensor.

The laptop did not leave its "sleep mode. "As I thought, it doesn't work. Let me try her right hand." She tried the first finger of the deceased's right hand, which also had no effect. She repeated the procedure on Feltham's smartphone, and no access was allowed to this device either.

Nick shook his head. "The cops in Bali may be able to access these devices, but we have no help between now and then. I'll check her backpack."

Blackman said, "She had a backpack?"

Nick looked about the cabin. "Yes. I saw her carrying it when we were refueling." He opened the cupboards in Feltham's Suite and located the small, black denim pack. He hesitated. "I don't want to contaminate any fingerprints or whatever."

Katie said, "I'll ask Marcia for some of those latex gloves they use when serving food."

A few minutes later, Nick opened the pack and found a wallet with credit cards, about two hundred dollars in cash, and Feltham's U.S. passport. The names matched. In addition, there was a clutch of paper printouts that he passed to Katie for review.

She read the various documents and let out a quiet whistle. "Wow. I think we've hit the jackpot."

Chapter Seven

Katie passed the documents to Nick, who perused them and passed them to Blackman. She took them back and selected one of the papers. "This first document is an official notification from the FBI. It says that, in return for her information regarding a major felony, the Feds will provide protection services for her. However, that is contingent on Ms. Feltham providing more evidence of the crime and its perpetrators."

Nick looked at Katie. "Do we know what the crime is?"

Katie scanned the other printouts. "The wording is somewhat vague, but it looks like she discovered a major fraud at BioContra. Some of the emails indicate that Feltham was an IT contractor for the company and came across something big and illegal. She had solid evidence on her laptop and seemed to have a plan to collect more. She indicates this would be by recording an interchange with one or more people from the company. The Feds asked her how she might do that, and she mentioned this flight to Bali."

Nick picked up on the story. "So, she wanted to be on the flight, corner one of the executives, and record the conversation. She would have used her smartphone. No wonder she seemed so pissed when the BioContra people were in the accident and missed the flight."

Katie held up another printout. "This is a final email to the Feds dated yesterday. She was convinced she was being followed, so she decided to follow her normal schedule, go to the gym to work out, and then leave directly to the airport."

Nick looked over the document. "Is fraud the motive? Did someone discover she was about to become a whistleblower to the Feds and decide to silence her?"

Blackman stood up. He had been listening intensely but had contributed nothing. "How could they kill her? All the BioContra people missed the flight."

⸻⟡⸻

Nick suggested that their first interview be with the man who knew most about the cause of death, Marcel Grange. As they had agreed, Blackman took charge and asked Marcia to bring the doctor to Business Class, where they had set up an area for the purpose. Most of the other passengers had changed their clothes into the airline's pajamas, and Dr. Grange was one of them.

Nick looked about him, and a smile spread over his lips. Katie, Ned, and he all wore identical blue pajamas. As did the doctor. *We look more like a group of prison inmates than an investigation team.*

The three interrogators had agreed on the questions that Blackman would ask, and, with a bit of prompting, he took the lead. "So, tell me, Doctor Grange, how come you're on this trip to Bali?" Nick switched on his smartphone's recorder app.

The doctor hesitated but said, "I'm visiting my son, Jimmy. He moved over there with his girlfriend. That was six months ago."

"Understood." Nick looked down at the notes he had taken previously and Blackman continued with his list of questions. Grange's answers confirmed the information they had already gathered but Blackman made a show of taking notes on a writing pad.

Katie raised another subject. "From the evidence we've found, it looks like BioContra may be involved in some sort of fraud. You work for a rival company in the same field. Can you guess what that fraud might be?"

The doctor almost smiled. "Interesting. Yes, I might be able to help. Just before the IPO, BioContra reported a major breakthrough in its research. But they were very mysterious about it and kept it secret even when their company went public. Their CFO projected a potentially huge gain in revenue and profits, and their stock price reflected the market's belief that the breakthrough was real. That would be fine, but if it's not legitimate, the stock would only be worth about 30% of what it traded is at."

As they were concluding their questions, the doctor raised an issue. "You shouldn't miss a significant point. I believe that the poison employed in Ms. Feltham's death was a cyanide solution. Cyanide is difficult to acquire. You can't buy it on Amazon, a regular pharmacy, or a hardware store. Whoever used it may have purchased it on the Dark Web, but BioContra uses it a lot, and many people in that company would have easy access to it."

Nick had been taking notes on his laptop but paused. "How certain are you that it was cyanide? Could it be some medication she was using? Could her death be an accident? Natural causes?"

"I have thirty years' experience dealing with poisons, and there are many telltale indicators. Her pallor. Her rigor mortis. The discoloration of her skin. The effect it had inside her nostril. The smell. I'm sure my diagnosis is correct."

Katie observed, "It was lucky we had you on the flight. Otherwise, the death would have gone down as natural until a postmortem, possibly in Indonesia. Or back in the States."

"Yes. An amazing coincidence," Nick added.

Doctor Grange understood the veiled insinuation but shrugged it off. He looked at Ned. "As well as having access to the poison, whoever was responsible had to load it into some delivery vehicle and cold-bloodedly administer it. You're the detective, but it sounds like a professional killer, not just another angry citizen. If I'm right, we have a very ruthless individual on board, and they represent an ongoing danger."

The doctor seemed to realize Nick and Katie had taken over the questioning rather than the homicide detective and frowned. However, he did not ask for an explanation, and when Blackman told him they were done, he appeared to notice that Blackman had looked to Katie for her agreement that their interview was finished.

When Grange returned to his Suite, Katie turned to Blackman. "You did well, Ned. That wasn't so hard, was it?"

⁘—⌇⌇⁚◯⁚⌇⌇—⁘

The team's following interview was with Anthony Stamford.

"Take a seat." Ned Blackman indicated where he wanted Stamford to sit. He added, "How are you taking it? Having a killer loose among us must be stressful."

"Damn right. It's scary. But you're the law here, so I expect you to protect me...and the others."

The venture capitalist was young and in his mid-thirties. *Another New Yorker* thought *Nick*. He wore a well-tailored dark blue suit with a white shirt and a red Italian silk tie. His shoes were brown suede loafers, *expensive*.

Ned started. "Thanks for meeting with us. Can you tell us a little about yourself?"

"Such as?"

Blackman read from his notepad. "Oh, the usual things. Where you live, what you do for a living, domestic arrangements."

Stamford grunted. "How is that relevant?"

Blackman stiffened but said sternly, "We'll decide what's relevant and what's not. Answer my question." Nick smiled in admiration for the security guard.

"I own a condo on the Upper West Side, am a venture capitalist, and have a live-in girlfriend. Anything else?" Stamford glared at each of the investigative team and added, "What's this all about? I came on this flight to enjoy myself, not be involved in some murder or other. I don't know anything about the woman or her death." He looked directly at Ned Blackman and gestured to Nick and Katie. "And why do you have these kids here?"

Katie pounced on him. "You were sitting in the same row as Ms. Feltham. You were opposite her, so you were certainly in a position to see what happened to her."

"I saw nothing. I watched a movie, and after that, I slept. I'll repeat. I saw nothing. Can I go now?"

Nick had already used the in-flight internet satellite connection to research the young man. He said, "You are to be congratulated, Mr. Stamford. I see you just made a fortune in the BioContra IPO."

Stamford frowned. "I did well. But I took some significant risks."

Nick continued. "You were the partner in your firm that spearheaded the early-stage investment. Is that right?"

"Yes. That's correct."

Ned read a question from his notepad. "You're traveling First Class now with the rest of us, but I'm surprised you booked a Business Class ticket. I'd have expected you would have purchased a First Class ticket."

The man appeared visibly shocked by his statement: "Just because I'm clever and worth a lot doesn't mean I throw money away."

Katie looked at the Armani suit he was wearing and picked up the questioning. "Taking a trip to Bali on the same flight as all the senior BioContra executives can't be just a coincidence."

"It's none of your business."

Ned, who, after his pre-defined questions had followed his typical pattern of remaining silent, seemed to wake up. "Mr. Stamford, this is a homicide investigation. In a few hours, you'll be asked the same questions by an Indonesian police officer, so I'd advise you to cooperate now. We may be able to save you some pain. *Comprende*?"

Stamford grunted his dissatisfaction but then answered Katie's question. "I've worked hard for BioContra, and with the IPO complete, I still have much to offer them. They'll need help on mergers and acquisitions, new funding efforts, and other investment banking matters. I can help them, and being on the Bali trip makes sense. It solidifies the relationship."

Katie jumped in. "Why Business Class?"

"Originally, I booked a First Class ticket, but then I realized that that would mean bumping one of the BioContra executives back to Business, so I changed it. Also, I didn't want them to think I was profiting too much from their IPO. Bad optics."

Katie looked at Nick, and his return expression confirmed that neither fully believed Stamford's explanation.

Stamford asked Ned, "Is there anything else?"

Nick looked at the venture capitalist. "You must be proud of your achievements. It's obvious that you're very successful. Must be an incredible story."

Stamford smiled. "Yes, I am proud. I decided early in life that setting a goal and then achieving it is what life is about."

Nick had personal experience with startup companies and smiled back, "Did you have a mission, a calling? Something that really excited you?"

"Only achieving my goal excited me."

"What was your goal?"

"To make a shitload of money. I'm currently worth over twenty million dollars."

Katie's dislike for the man intensified. "I guess you've had to bend a few rules to make that."

"Whatever it took."

Katie dropped the bombshell. "Did you know the FBI is investigating a fraud accusation against BioContra?"

Stamford turned pale but recovered quickly. "I'm not surprised. Whenever someone is successful, envy creeps in. The Feds always want to make a name for themselves. I'll wager that there'll be nothing to it when the smoke clears."

Katie said quietly, "But if there is, you and your net worth would take a hit. Right?"

"It's not a big deal. Now, if there is nothing more…"

Nick shook his head, and Ned said to the venture capitalist, "You can go."

The man gave him a sneer, rose, and returned to his Suite.

Nick affected a breezy smile. "Who's next?"

Chapter Eight

One of Pacifico Airlines' differentiating features was its cross-ocean internet access, which was incorporated into its small fleet of aircraft. Though many of the airline's competitors provided a similar service, most were poor, particularly when flying over long stretches of water, such as the Pacific Ocean. The Pacifico system accessed all satellite service suppliers and continually switched carriers to use the best signal available.

Nick found it far from perfect, but he had been able to research areas where he had questions, including Anthony Stamford's role in the BioContra IPO. He was also able to send and receive emails. Consulting his smartwatch, he saw that it was 8:00 AM Eastern time, so his email requests had a reasonable chance of yielding replies within the next few hours. His spreadsheet analyzing each of the passengers and crew also required checking some of the details of their stories, and he spent time accessing their profiles and posts on LinkedIn, Instagram, TikTok, and Facebook. "Wow. That's interesting." He called to Katie's Suite. "Come over and see this."

They were sharing the tasks, and she put down her laptop and joined him. "What have you got?"

He showed her a TikTok video of a party with four or five people of Nick's and Katie's age, dancing and singing one of the latest pop songs.

Katie asked, "What's that?"

"As the caption says, that is Jimmy Grange, the doctor's son."

"So?"

"So, the video was made just a week ago in a Manhattan bar. Why is Grange going to Bali to visit his son when his son is in New York?"

Marcia Krebs had been a flight attendant for eight years. Pacifico was a dream job compared to the previous airline she worked for. She now dealt with wealthier passengers and found them less demanding and less stressed by the flying experience. She was approaching thirty years of age and thought back to the early days when she had loved the travel, the new cities and countries and the image of worldliness. She aspired to meet a sophisticated passenger and marry him. This had not transpired, and the gypsy life, often on call and most nights spent away from her home, did not provide a basis for a serious liaison outside her airline job. She had decided that on her thirtieth birthday, she would quit and find other employment.

The death of Trisha Feltham had rattled her. It was bad enough that a passenger had died on the flight, but the doctor seemed sure that this was a murder, and that the killer was still loose. She was sure it was one of the passengers, but which one? Perhaps she should bring forward her decision to leave the airline industry.

She thought about the couple in Row 2. She admired what she knew of Nick and Katie and believed their relationship would last for life. Both were well-balanced and sane individuals—an equal partnership and two people obviously in love. Many people would view Nick and Katie's relationship with jealousy, but Marcia saw it as inspirational.

Her mind shifted to Ned Backman. She was suspicious of the New York detective. Marcia knew little about policework, but her observation told her that Blackman seemed less competent than he should be. *I should convey my views to Katie,* she thought.

The investigative team had given her a task while they were interviewing the passengers. They instructed her, "Search for anything that might be relevant, particularly the murder weapon?"

Having spent significant time in Feltham's cabin, she had found nothing new, and the principal object of her hunt - whatever was used to disburse the poison – had eluded her.

A thought hit her—the trash bins! She had already searched the bin in the forward bathroom, so she would now check out those in the galley.

She had pulled on latex gloves and started searching, sifting through the paper and trash in the bins. She discovered nothing. Her failure to locate something relevant frustrated her, and on a whim, she decided to be doubly sure about the one up front. She had not found anything the first time, but now her hand grasped something small and rigid plastic. She fetched it out and looked at what she recognized as a nasal spray bottle. She shook it gently and confirmed that it contained a little liquid.

She had not secured the bathroom door and was surprised when it was pushed open. Teresa Holmes stood outside looking in. "Oh," she said, "I didn't know it was occupied."

Marcia blushed. "I'm sorry. Just searching. I should have locked it."

"Find anything?"

"Yes. I think so." She held up the bottle.

"May I see it?" Holmes reached out her hand.

"No. I can't do that. From what I'm told, this is probably the murder weapon."

Teresa Holmes stepped back, raising her hands to shield herself from the repugnant sight. "God. How awful."

Marcia walked rapidly away towards the back of the plane and, meeting up with Blackman, offered him what she had found. He was about to take it but stopped himself. "Maybe fingerprints," he muttered. Marcia looked at him, thinking, *Of course, there might be. Some detective you are!*

Nick looked at the bottle. "Certainly, it looks like what you'd expect the weapon to be. Where did you find it?"

"In the bathroom up front."

Katie was puzzled. "But you looked there before."

"I did, and it wasn't there then."

Nick nodded. "The murderer must have kept it with them to dispose of when we arrive in Bali. But when Grange identified the cause of death and likely weapon, they decided to get rid of it rather than have it found on them, if searched."

⁂

The team interviewed Ken Grobe next.

Nick led off. "You make a great cocktail, Ken."

"Thanks. I'm proud of that. Before this job, I was a mixologist in Atlanta. I worked in a swanky establishment, and, as in most restaurants, the main profit-maker was the bar. Another bartender and I developed a range of specialty cocktails and modeled ourselves on the guys in the movie *Cocktail.* Pacifico Airlines wanted differentiated skills on their planes and chose me and others like me for their First Class bars. They trained us in all the other stuff about being flight attendants, but they were looking for barmen that passengers would remember."

"You like the work?"

"Absolutely. I don't have a girlfriend back home, and I get to see the world. Nice places, nice hotels, nice food." He added, "I don't know how long I'll do it, but I can't imagine a better job just now."

Nick switched to the investigation. "Think back to around midnight Pacific time. What were you doing then?"

Ken answered after a moment's pause. "Everyone had left the bar and returned to their seats. I was clearing up, washing stemware, and putting the liquors away. I walked through to see if anyone had empty glasses or trash. Most passengers were asleep, but a few were watching movies or reading."

"Did you notice Trisha Feltham?"

"I did. She was sitting up in her bed with her laptop out. I think she was about to send off an email. She asked Marcia how to get on the internet to do that."

Nick addressed Katie and Ned. "That was when I was settling down."

Ken nodded. "Yes. I recall asking you if you had any trash."

Nick became excited. "Just after that, I heard a commotion in the Suite behind mine. Feltham's. That was probably when the murder occurred. Did you see anything else?"

"No." He paused and his eyes opened wide. "But, now I think about it, yes. I'm sure that one passenger was walking about. I can't place who it was. It was dark, and everyone was wearing pajamas. They all looked the same, and to be honest, I wasn't paying much attention."

"Try to remember. That person might be the murderer."

Before Grobe could reply, the captain's voice, in its clipped speech, resounded over the speaker system. "Ladies, gentlemen, we shortly experiencing turbulence that could be severe so return to Suites and ensure seatbelts tightly fastened. Cabin crew, secure aircraft, and take seats."

Marcia appeared. "Sounds like it's going to be rough. Let's move."

The investigative team quickly returned to their Suites and tighened their seat belts. Marcia and Jeff checked that all the passengers were secure and took their seats at the front of the plane. Ken sprinted to the bar and stowed most of the bottles and glassware before joining them.

Minutes later, the A320 bucked as it encountered the first wave of turbulence. Katie looked out of her cabin window at the dark sky and the rivers of rain running across the glass. The A320 lurched to the right and then to the left.

"Oh my God. We're going to die." Teresa shouted out what everyone was thinking.

The turbulence continued but then eased a little, and Teresa became the passengers' most vocal thought again. "That's better."

Suddenly, the plane started to drop like an elevator whose cable had snapped. Katie's eyes opened wide but she did not speak. Nick, from across the aisle, let out an expletive. The dramatic change in air current had resulted in the aircraft descending nearly five thousand feet in seconds. A collection of personal items flew into the air and crashed against the ceiling. The passengers cried out in fear, and the captain fought to regain control of the airplane. The Pratt & Whitney engines screamed as the captain attempted to halt the airplane's descent.

His efforts finally succeeded, and the plane leveled out at 33,000 feet. Backpacks, smartphones, and tablets rained down, and several passengers became nauseous and reached for airsick bags.

Further severe rocking and rapid changes in altitude lasted for another five minutes, but a period of calm followed with only minor disturbances. The passengers and crew sat silent, waiting for a potential recurrence, fearing for their lives.

"Is it over?" Again, Teresa Holmes became the mouthpiece for everyone's thoughts.

"This is captain. We are clear and I now climb to regain original altitude of 38,000 feet. I ran tests on aircraft, and so far, seems good. I will run more tests but until we are on ground, some things cannot be checked. We cannot land before Denpasar, so we continue to our destination. I will advise if anything else happen. Flight attendants, check passengers." The cabin crew understood that his request meant for them to check the passengers for injuries.

Jeff Stokes surveyed the cabin. It was a mess with personal items, books, a few glasses, pillows, and blankets strewn about. He barked instructions, and the crew freed themselves from their seat belts and spread out to inquire about the passengers. The flight attendant who had joined in Los Angeles, Sharon Brown, had not secured her shoulder harness correctly, and when the plane dropped, she strained against the seat and suffered damage to her right arm.

"I think my arm is broken. I'll stay here until you check everyone else."

Stokes started in the first row.

Teresa Holmes was ashen. "God! I thought I was going to die."

"Are you alright?"

"I'm bruised from the seatbelt, but since it saved my life, I bear it no ill will." She laughed nervously. "I said I wanted an adventure, but a murder and a near crash? That's going to extremes."

Two or three passengers headed to the bathrooms, and Ken went to his bar to check the damage. It was a mess. Despite his efforts before the turbulence, there were a dozen or so shattered bottles and a significant number of broken glasses.

It took Jeff Stokes ten minutes to meet with each passenger and direct his cabin crew to assist those who needed help. Jim Borders had a bruise from where his backpack had fallen on him, and Marcia provided him with an icepack. Anthony Stamford was missing.

Marcia asked, "Anyone seen Mr. Stamford?"

The doctor, having previously made it clear that he did not like the venture capitalist, told Stokes. "He went back to the bathroom in Business Class. I reckon he soiled himself."

"Are you alright, doctor?"

"Sort of, Marcia. I threw up but managed to use the bag."

"Let me take that from you and get you some water. Sharon Brown was hurt. Can you look at her for me?"

"Of course."

Jeff Stokes made his way to the bar and saw smashed bottles and glassware. He shook his head, but then his face registered surprise. *Where is Ken? He should be back here cleaning up the mess, but he is nowhere in sight. Bathroom? And where is Stamford?*

He looked towards the back of the plane and spotted the venture capitalist returning from one of the bathrooms at the rear. They met. "Are you okay, sir?"

Stamford snarled, "Your stupid captain couldn't control his aircraft, and he ruined a very expensive suit."

Stokes noticed his trousers were wet, probably having been removed and sponged out. "Can I get you anything, sir?"

"A new Armani would be nice." Stamford pushed past him and returned to his Suite.

The Passenger Service Manager stood in front of the bar, looked around, and said out loud. "Damned you, Ken. Where are you? Well, I'd better start clearing this up myself. Where is he?" Then, he saw something that made him pause. Protruding from the side of the bar was a foot. It was not moving.

Jeff Stokes moved to a position where he could look behind the bar and saw the blood-stained body of Ken Grobe. "Oh, shit."

Chapter Nine

The barman lay on his back with rugged cuts across his throat. His open, lifeless eyes had a look of surprise, and he gazed toward the ceiling. A broken bottle was next to the body, and Stokes saw that the sharp edges at its base matched the gashes in Ken's throat. Perhaps it was an accident from a smashed bottle, but it was more likely another murder.

The Passenger Service Manager called into the First Class cabin area. "Doctor Grange. We have an emergency here."

Grange had returned from treating Sharon and joined the Passenger Service Manager.

Stokes asked him, "Is he dead?"

After a brief examination, the doctor nodded. "I'm afraid he is." He added, "This doesn't look like an accident. I'll call Ned Blackman."

Two minutes later, Blackman stood before the corpse and shook his head. "This is now a crime scene. Please give me a few moments and ask Nick and Katie to join me."

When they met, Katie looked at the broken bottle. "There's blood smeared all over the neck. If someone used it as a weapon to kill him, that's where they would have held it. The blood will have destroyed any fingerprints."

Nick peered closely at what was probably the murder weapon. "The other bottles flew up to the ceiling and smashed either there or when the captain regained control of the plane, and they fell to the floor." He turned. "They have all shattered, whereas the bottle that killed him is intact, other than at the base. I think the killer broke it on the counter and then used it on our friendly bartender." He looked at the end of the bar and saw an indentation that corroborated his hypothesis.

Ned asked, "Why kill Ken? He was just a barman."

Nick regarded the corpse. "True but think back. Just before the turbulence, he was talking about seeing someone up and about at the time of Fetham's death. He couldn't remember who it was at the time."

Jeff Stokes had left them and informed the captain of Ken's death, and the two of them rushed back to the bar area.

The captain took charge. "What happen?"

Nick signaled to Blackman, who, haltingly, described what they knew so far and the fact that the death was likely another murder.

"This not good. Let me think one minute."

They waited for Silofski to continue.

"Stokes, put in a body bag and stow in back. Passengers may panic so I make announcement. Reassure them no more murders. I hope no more murders." He let out a sharp breath and continued. "Have Marcia prepare hot food. Soup if you have. I know Sharon is injured but she must help. All passengers now remain in Suites. Serve food and drinks there. Safer this way."

Blackman started to shake. "Perhaps we ought to stop the investigation. I don't think we should put others at risk. Let's leave it to the Indonesians."

Katie glared at him. "It's not going to happen. We have a professional killer on board, and he probably has an escape plan for when we reach Denpasar. We must catch him before we land and have the captain take him into custody."

Silofski nodded. "I agree, Ms. Bunn."

Ned shuddered. "So, what do we do next?"

Katie answered him. "We have to continue our efforts while broadening it to take Ken's death into account."

Nick looked down at the body. "We still have a few people to interview. Let's do Jim Borders. Is that okay, Captain?"

Silofski looked at Blackman, who nodded in agreement. "Da. But everyone stays in Suites unless being interviewed or part your team, Detective Blackman."

⁕⁓ᦞᧉⵔ()ᦞᧉ⵫⁓⁕

Katie accessed their spreadsheet and reviewed what they knew about the roofing contractor. It was not much. Borders had been open about his company but less about his private life.

She thought there was something more to his relationship with this wife and commented to Nick and Blackman, "He likes to ask direct, sometimes abusive, questions and is happy to talk about his business. But didn't you say he was defensive when you asked him about his home life?"

Her husband replied, "Yes, that's right. When I asked about his wife, he turned away before answering. I think that's a tell. When he does that, he's lying."

Marcia escorted Borders to the back of the plane to face Nick, Katie, and Ned Blackman. Jim Borders appeared to be suffering from the excessive drinking he had indulged in earlier in the flight coupled with the near crash of the aircraft. He was not in a good mood. "I understand you have another bloody death on your hands."

Blackman said, "That's what it looks like."

Katie looked at the roofing contractor. "How are you taking it? It's clear we have a killer among us, and most of the passengers are close to panic. But, you seem very calm."

"There's no one here that I'm worried by. I could take any one of them on and beat the shit out of them. I have no fear of this killer." Borders slumped down in a seat. "Anyway, you're wasting your time with me. I didn't see anything before the woman's death. She was two rows behind me. As far as Ken goes, I saw him return to the bar after the turbulence ended. Nothing else."

Nick prompted Ned, who read a question from his notepad. "Maybe not, but what did you do immediately after the turbulence subsided?"

Borders's blunt manner intensified. "This is bullshit. I'll bet that you've got it all screwed up. I'll bet that the techie woman wasn't even murdered.

Grange doesn't seem that smart to me. He's probably got it wrong, and the woman died of drugs or something."

Nick interrupted. "And Ken?"

"That is a real shame. He was a fabulous barman. But I'll wager he was killed accidentally during the turbulence."

Blackman said nothing.

Katie looked Borders in the eyes. "Can you tell us a little more about you?"

"I told you before. I'm a roofing contractor."

Sensing that the man had an issue with Katie questioning him, Nick signaled her that he would take over. "Your job must be a tough one. I guess it's stressful dealing with lots of projects and lots of hourly workers. Many of your workers are probably not the brightest."

"Yes. It's demanding work. But I've got it cracked. My men accept that I am the alpha male. What I say goes. No second guessing. If they don't buy that, they're fired."

Nick followed up. "Does Mrs. Borders feel the same way?"

He looked away, "She knows her place."

Silence descended on the group, which Nick broke. "That you're the alpha male?"

"Correct. You kids might think it's old-fashioned, but I earn the money and expect her to understand. Simple, isn't it?"

Katie could not help herself. "Sounds like she would have enjoyed a trip to Bali."

"I'm going there to have fun. If my wife were with me, I would be miserable."

Again, silence descended until Borders spoke. He looked directly at Katie. "If you must know, the marriage is broken. Has been for years. I drink too much, and she keeps nagging me about it. It might be different if she was more fun to be with."

He stood up and paced a little. "Anyway, I'm fed up with your questioning. The big detective from New York doesn't seem to have any questions, and you two kids are interrogating me. I don't get it."

After the roofing contractor returned to his seat, Katie asked Nick, "New subject. From what you found, Grange lied to us. Why would he do that?"

"Let's ask him."

Katie suggested, "Let me take the lead."

"Okay, by me."

Blackman said nothing.

They walked to the doctor's Suite, and Katie knocked politely on the partition. Grange looked up from a book he was reading and asked, "How can I help? Not another body, I hope." He maintained his characteristic severe expression.

Katie led off. "You told us you were traveling to Bali to meet up with your son."

"That's right."

"So, your son has been in Bali for months? Six months?"

"Er. Yes."

"Odd. A recent TikTok video clearly shows him partying in New York."

"Oh."

"Why did you lie?"

The doctor's expression became distorted. "Actually, I'm meeting someone else there."

"Go on."

"A lady."

"Not your wife."

"Correct."

"Why lie?"

"It was a personal matter. Why would I share that with strangers?"

"Okay. Ordinarily, this wouldn't matter, but as you well know, we have two murders on our hands. You can see that we need to follow up on all leads or inconsistencies."

"You can't be accusing me. If I were the killer, I would have told you Feltham's death was from a heart attack or other natural causes. You wouldn't be having this investigation."

"Point taken."

Grange had appeared to be a humorless man and now his facade seemed to crack. "You two seem to have an important thing in common."

Nick was puzzled. "What's that got to do with it?"

"You are both intelligent. You match each other, which bodes well for a long life together. I'm not handsome, and I met my wife many years ago. She was beautiful and still is. I couldn't believe that she was interested in me. I thought I was lucky, but she was not very bright. She only wants to discuss her clothes, makeup, beauty treatments, and workouts. Her only asset is a perfect body. We have nothing in common. I need what you two have—

an intellectual match. The woman I'm meeting in Bali is not as beautiful as my wife, but we already have a deeper relationship. I don't know how this'll turn out, but I know I must move on from my marriage."

He looked at Katie and then at Nick. "I'll say it again. You two have got it made."

Ned Blackman said nothing, and Nick turned to him. "Any further questions, Ned?"

"Er. No."

After they left the doctor's Suite, Katie asked Blackman, "What do you think? Is he the killer?"

"How would I know?"

Nick was becoming annoyed by Ned's seeming reluctance to be involved. "You must have an opinion."

"Not really."

Katie looked at their spreadsheet. "Who's next?"

Nick answered her. "Let's switch a little. We've concentrated on the passengers so far. What about the crew?"

He looked over Katie's shoulder at her laptop screen. "We have the cockpit crew – two pairs of pilots - and the cabin crew – Jeff and his flight attendants. What do we know about the pilots?"

Blackman, at last, volunteered something. "The pilots changed out at about 1:00 AM Pacific Time, about three hours after the murder. That means Reynolds and Gonzales were flying the plane, and Silofski and Parsons were resting at the time of death."

Katie said, "I guess we can take Reynolds and Gonzales off the suspect list."

"But not Silofski and his first officer. What's his name?" Nick consulted his notes. "There it is. The co-pilot is Parsons, Rob Parsons."

She nodded. "Let's start with him."

A few minutes later, Parsons left the flight deck and met with the team.

Katie started. "You were in the rest area with Captain Silofski. Did either of you leave during that time?"

Parsons thought for a moment. "I did not. We both had dinner in LA prior to the flight departing and when we boarded, we came to the back to rest. I was fast asleep most of the time. But I did hear the captain leaving his bunk. He walked forward towards the First Class cabin."

"What time was that?"

"I'm not sure. I went back to sleep, but it was before midnight Pacific time. We changed shifts with Captain Reynolds at 1:00 AM."

Parsons answered a few more questions and then Nick asked about something that had been on his mind. "You were on the flight deck when Captain Silofski was advised of Ms. Feltham's death?"

"Yes."

"Even when the captain learned that the death was probably a murder, he decided to fly on to Bali rather than divert to Hawaii. Why did he do that?"

"I don't know. We were well north of there, and there would have been a major disruption to our schedule. But you'll have to ask him that?"

At the mention of Hawaii, Nick's thoughts returned to a trip that Katie and he had taken there just sixteen months before. It was there, while swimming that Nick revealed a ring hidden in the sea and asked her to become his wife. He smiled at the memory.

Ten minutes later, Captain Silofski sat uneasily as Blackman started the questioning. "Where were you when the murder took place."

Silofski sneered, "Where you think I was? I was flying plane."

Katie interrupted. "You were flying the plane when Trisha Feltham's death was discovered, but the murder occurred three hours before while you were still resting in the back."

Blackman consulted his notepad and asked a question he had agreed with Nick and Katie. "Why did you decide to fly to Bali when we could have easily diverted to Hawaii?"

Silofski's face hardened, and he answered quietly, "I consult with bosses by radio, and they decide."

Katie said, "Did they give you a reason? Nick plotted our position. When you knew there was a death on board, we were north of the islands, and you could have swung south and landed there."

"Not my decision. But red tape in Honolulu would be bad. Costly land there too. Easier fly on to Bali."

"Did the red tape and extra cost contribute to the decision?"

"How would I know? I not make decision. That was base. Management made decision."

Nick added, "Actually, without Dr. Grange, we'd have assumed she died of natural causes. Hell, how can you murder someone on a plane? If we landed in Honolulu, the authorities might have discovered it was a homicide. In Denpasar, that discovery would be less likely. Any views on that, captain?"

"What you accuse me?"

Katie looked up from her keyboard. "We are accusing you of nothing. Just asking some questions."

"I not understand." He pointed to Blackman. "This man is detective but you two ask most questions. Is he in charge? Is this clever *Columbo*-type interrogation?"

Katie sensed an issue and quickly attempted to change Silofski's line of thought. "Your First Officer mentioned that you left the rest area at the back of the plane at about the time of the murder."

"I go for pee. That is not crime."

"Your co-pilot says you walked forward. Why not use the bathrooms at the back of the plane?"

Silofski paused before replying, "I went stretch my legs." The captain gave out a laugh. "So detectives, do you think same murderer killed passenger and Ken?"

Nick answered for the team. "Yes. That's logical."

The captain smiled. "Then not me. When Ken killed, I flying plane through turbulence and after. You remember?"

Chapter Ten

This is so exciting." Teresa Holmes greeted the investigators with a smile. "I've lived in New York for fifty years and never been involved in a murder before. And now, two murders and a near crash. I knew this trip would be exciting, but not like this."

Ned gestured to a seat, and Teresa sank into it.

"How are you coping, Ms. Holmes."

"Please, call me Teresa." She paused but said, "I ought to be scared to death…" She realized her choice of words was poor and followed up by saying. "Most passengers are close to panic but are trying to show a brave face. I see it all as an adventure. Just as we could have all been killed in the turbulence, the killer might want to kill all of us. My life has been very boring until this trip and I am 73. I want to enjoy myself."

Nick asked, "You're traveling alone on the flight. Meeting someone in Bali?"

"I hope so."

After leaving LA, Teresa had changed into a set of pajamas, as had most of the passengers, but Katie observed she had shed these and reverted to her original clothes. Katie, responding to her flippant nature in the shadow of two murders, gave her an admonishing look. The woman noticed Katie's look and said, "Somehow, the murders made me want to get out of those pajamas." Her face twisted as she recognized the seriousness of the conversation, and she followed up. "I'm sure you want to know more about me."

Nick took over the questioning. "That would be helpful."

"Okay. I married early, and my husband insisted I quit my job and become a full-time housewife. We had one child, a girl, but she was killed in a car accident when she was only eighteen. We were married for nearly fifty years, then he died a month ago."

She had been sitting but now stood and faced the team. "He was one of those old-fashioned types and wanted me to stay at home, prepare his dinner punctually every night, and manage the household. We lived together all our years in Manhattan. It was one of the old buildings, but it was nice. We had central AC, an elevator, and a doorman." She paused before adding, "My husband was kind and generous, but he saw me as an appendage. Before our marriage, I worked as a secretary in a law firm, but as soon as the wedding was over, he insisted I give up work. I could have done so much more with my life. I might have even completed a law degree and become a lawyer. I envy you two. Both smart. Both young and I'd guess both with careers and able to make the most of your lives."

Nick was about to interrupt her, but Katie flashed him a signal to let Teresa Holmes complete her monologue.

"He left me more than comfortable, so I decided that I was going to see the world. He took me on a few of his business trips to Europe in the early days but never to Asia. The idea of flying to Bali seemed a good start to the rest of my life. And being upgraded was the cherry on top of the cake."

"What did your husband do?"

"It's funny, but I don't know. He traveled a lot and said he was in sales but never talked about his job. He had projects that took him away for a month or two—or even three. And after that, he would have a month or two at home. He never went to an office."

Nick and Katie had empathetic accuracy, enabling them to read each other's thoughts, and they looked at each other. *The late Mr. Holmes lived a life consistent with that of a contract killer.* They saw Teresa smiling at them. *Is she playing with us? Has she inherited the family business? Is she now a killer? Were she and her husband a team?*

After Teresa returned to her Suite, Katie made a suggestion. "We've interviewed everyone now, so let's pause and take stock."

Blackman nodded. "I need to go to the bathroom. Let's take a ten-minute break."

Nick answered for Katie and him. "Sounds like a plan. Back here in ten."

Ned departed, and Nick looked at Katie. "Alone at last." He reached over, and they kissed.

"Sorry to butt in." It was Marcia.

Katie smiled. "Hi, Marcia. How are you doing? We haven't spoken since Ken…" She left the sentence unfinished.

Tears rolled down her face. "I'm so upset. I didn't know Ken that well, but he was a nice man and very talented. Why would someone do something like this? And who did it?"

Nick put his hand on her shoulder. "That's what we're trying to find out."

Marcia's face turned from tears to one of rage. "I'll bet that detective isn't much help."

Katie looked at her. "What do you mean?"

"He doesn't seem to know anything about police work. When I've been around, and you've been interviewing people, you seem to be asking the questions, not him. I don't get it."

Katie nodded. "I understand. And we agree with you. Let's say we have a plan and a methodology that's working so far. Please trust us. We have this under control."

"Okay. I don't know what you're up to, but I have confidence in you. Thanks. Please find the scumbag who killed Ken."

Blackman returned, and they started their review. Both Nick and Katie had the synchronized spreadsheet open on their laptops.

Katie opened the conversation. "We're facing a cold-blooded murderer who will stop at nothing to avoid detection. Ken found that to his cost."

Nick added, "The killer's use of the cyanide spray on Feltham indicates that the crime was premeditated and points to a contract killer."

Katie asked, "Motive?"

Nick was quick to answer. "We don't have proof, but it seems probable that BioContra has a lot to gain from the death of their whistleblower. And they would have access to the poison. As Doctor Grange pointed out, cyanide is not easy to purchase."

Blackman seemed to become more energized. "We have two suspects who have obvious links to BioContra. The venture capitalist is one, and Grange works for a major competitor of the company."

"That doesn't mean that either of them is the killer. If the murderer is a professional, his real client may not even be on the plane. Perhaps he's one of those eighty or so stranded on their way to Kennedy."

Blackman contributed, "I wonder if missing the flight was accidental or it was part of the plan."

"Who knows?"

Nick said, "Let's take each of our suspects in turn. We'll start with passengers in Row 1." He looked down at his laptop. "Suite 1A is Jim Borders, the roofing contractor. Physically, he fits my picture of a contract killer. He could have committed both murders. He complained about a bruise he said he suffered from his backpack falling on him, but that was after the turbulence subsided. According to Marcia, he was one of the first up afterward and rushed to the bathroom."

Katie asked, "Front or back bathrooms?"

"She can't remember. She thinks the front, but most people needed to go, and when the front one was occupied, some went back to the two in Business Class. There was a lot of confusion, but Marcia believes Borders used the forward bathroom."

Katie referenced the next entry in the spreadsheet. "Suite 1B is Teresa Holmes. Lovely old lady, but that might be a front. Despite her age, she is strong enough to commit both crimes, and poison is traditionally a female weapon."

Nick laughed. "Her story sounded more like her late husband was the hitman. But, they may have been a team."

Katie picked up the analysis. "Row 2 – Nick and Katie. The newlyweds hit team?" Ned looked at the two of them and showed his surprise.

"Just joking, Ned."

Nick looked at the sheet. "Row 3 – 3A. Anthony Stamford. He seems fixated on making money, but that might be a cover. However, I checked him out on LinkedIn, and he appears to be what he says he is. I sent a few emails to people I know who might know more about him. It's still early morning in New York, so I haven't heard back. He might have access to the poison through his dealings with BioContra, and he was certainly at the back of the plane after the turbulence. He could have killed Ken on his way. Maybe washing his clothes, which Jeff told us about, was to remove blood stains."

Katie added some notes and then said, "4A. Doctor Grange. It's unlikely to be him. He pointed out that Feltham's death was not natural. But he did lie to us about why he was taking this trip. When we caught him, he came up with an excuse about a mistress, but who knows?"

Nick nodded. "Jim Borders made an interesting point about him. It was Grange who identified the poison and that it was a homicide. But we only have his word on that. Could he have a motive to call it something that it wasn't? Maybe it wasn't a murder after all."

Katie followed up. "But we do have the inhaler. Or, at least, an inhaler. And our murderer did kill Ken."

"An act of desperation."

"What about the crew?"

Nick shook his head. "I don't think it could be any of them. If the killer is a professional, he wouldn't be tied down in a full-time job that continually takes them across the world and doesn't allow them freedom of movement. Also, the use of the cyanide spray needed planning. I'm pretty sure that crew assignments are decided short-term. It wouldn't have been possible to plan for the killer to be on this specific flight. Also, one cockpit crew was flying the plane when the first murder took place while Silofski and Parsons were sleeping in the back. The second was while Silofski was flying the plane. We don't have a good reason for Silofski deciding to skip landing in Hawaii, but…"

Nick suddenly stood, started to pace the aisle, and looked puzzled. Katie asked him, "What's up? You seem to have thought of something."

"That's the problem. I'm missing something. There's something I am trying to remember. Something happened, or someone said something important, but I can't place it."

Ned Blackman interrupted Nick's thought. "Don't forget me. I'm a suspect as well. I did lie to you about being a cop."

Chapter Eleven

Silofski's Russian accent punctuated the air. "Hello again. This is captain. We have just two hours' flight time to Bali and will be arriving on time at 5:00 AM local. Having crossed International Date Line, you have lost one day."

Nick saw a notification on his laptop. It indicated the arrival of inbound emails replying to queries he had sent several hours before. The first three were from friends in venture capital and private equity firms. The message from each was similar. Anthony Stamford was successful but not universally trusted and frequently operated in a legally gray area. Nothing new, but they confirmed Nick's view of the man. Others also validated some of the stories from other passengers that Ned,

Katie, and he had been fed. One corroborated that airline management had decided to have Silofski bypass Hawaii.

Nick's eyes fixed on the next two, which related to one specific individual. The first confirmed what Nick expected, but the second was a surprise. Then, he remembered what had been worrying him for several hours.

He joined Katie in her Suite and told her what he had found.

She shook her head. "Of course. It makes sense. So, what do we do now?"

"There's one more thing I want to check," Nick said. He asked to speak with the captain over the plane's intercom system. The captain agreed to his request and directed Nick's call to the Pacifico central booking office.

After the call, Nick gave Katie a dry smile. "I guess that confirms it. But, if I'm right and we confront him, he'll deny it and spin another yarn."

Katie said, "Or he may just kill us."

Nick sat down on Katie's "guest seat". "Shall we do the Hercule Poirot thing? Gather everyone together and announce the killer's name?"

Katie sighed. "A bit too dramatic for me. Let's recruit one or two able-bodied people who can take him down if he gives us any trouble. Why not get them to meet us in the bar."

"I'll have the captain okay that."

Ten minutes later, they found that most of the suspects had moved to the bar and sat there as Jeff had taken over bartending duties. Ken's body had been moved to the back of the plane next to Trisha Feltham. Jeff and Marcia had finished cleaning up the debris from the turbulence, and the bar was clean and fresh. It looked no different to an outside observer than before the near-catastrophic incident. Nick and Katie had changed out of their pajamas and noticed everyone else had followed Teresa's example and done the same.

Blackman sat at the bar with the rest, and Borders turned to him. "Well, Ned, did you catch the murderer?"

Blackman seemed to relax. "No. We didn't, and with just a couple of hours left, I reckon it'll be up to the Indonesian police to conduct a full investigation."

Jeff stood behind the bar with Marcia and asked for orders. "I'm not a bartender, so I can't offer you specialty cocktails. But I can do the simple stuff. What can I get you?"

Nick, a registered bartender from his college days, stopped himself from volunteering to help out.

Through bleary eyes, Borders asked, "What time is it?"

Jeff replied, "It's four PM Eastern, one PM Pacific, and three AM in Bali."

Borders made up his mind. "Well, it's five o'clock somewhere. Give me a bourbon, Jeff. With what's been going on, make it a large one."

"Coming right up." Reaching for a bottle that had not been damaged, Jeff turned to Ned Blackman. "And for you, sir?"

"Just two more hours. Damn it. I'll have a champagne. The good stuff."

After pouring Borders' bourbon, Jeff selected a chilled bottle of champagne from the wine store. "It's a 2013 Dom Perignon. Will that do you?"

Ned nodded, and Jeff uncorked the bottle and poured a measure into a flute.

Ned took the glass by the stem, held it to the light, and then sniffed it gently. "An excellent year. Nectar of the Gods."

Nick commented, "I didn't think you knew your champagnes that well."

"Oh, I don't. I've seen people do that, you know, sniffing the wine."

"And you're holding the glass the way you should—by the stem—not the way a homicide detective from New York might hold it."

Blackman immediately shifted his grip to the one he had used previously, as you would a beer. "You forget, Nick, I'm not NYPD."

Only Nick and Katie knew this, and the others gasped.

Nick turned to them. "Katie and I have a confession to make."

Grange smirked, breaking his serious expression for, perhaps, the first time. "I've got it. You and your lovely new bride, did it? You two are the killers?"

Nick and Katie laughed in unison. "No. But we did deceive you. Ned Blackman is not a homicide detective. We found out when we were in L.A. He tells us he is a building security guard."

"You've been conning us all this time?" Anthony Stamford was confused and angry. He turned to Ned. "What right did you have to question me?" He switched his gaze to Nick and Katie. "And what right did you two have?"

Nick and Katie ignored him, but they could see that all the men seated at the bar were outraged that they had been misled.

The cabin lights had been dimmed for most of the flight, and Teresa Holmes emerged from the gloom. "Gosh. Everyone's here. Hello boys. Is this a guy-only party, or may a little old lady join you?"

Katie shrugged. All the passengers were now assembled. "I guess this is a Hercule Poirot moment after all. Lady and gentlemen, we want to update you on the case."

Nick took the floor. "Something new has come up. I made some email inquiries hours ago but only just received replies."

Stamford sipped from the glass of single malt Scotch that Jeff had poured him. "Damned kids again. Damned lying kids."

Katie glared at him. "The emails about you were not very complementary. And they hinted that you may be involved in the fraud at BioContra."

The venture capitalist gulped, and Nick continued. "However, no one I communicated with thought you would commit murder. People commented on your physical squeamishness."

Nick turned to face the fake policeman. "Ned, I checked you out with the Precinct, and they confirmed you did not work there."

"So what? I told you that already."

"I also contacted the security firm you told us you worked for. They've never heard of you either."

All eyes were now on Ned Blackman. "And by the way, a security guard is even less likely to know about vintage champagne than a homicide detective."

"So, you've caught me lying twice, and you don't like the way I hold a champagne glass. If you're accusing me of murder, you'll need something more than that."

Nick changed the subject. "You didn't have much contact with the victim until after her death. Right, Ned?"

"No. I didn't."

"Then, how did you know she was left-handed? When we tried to access her laptop and phone, you volunteered that gem of information."

Blackman was flustered but said, "It was a lucky guess."

Katie now picked up the story. "And you were the only one, other than Nick and I, who knew about Ken trying to remember who he had seen at the time of the murder."

Blackman's demeanor changed. Throughout the flight, he had appeared dithering and pathetic, but now he stood up straight. "You have no proof and no jurisdiction. When we reach Denpasar, I'll walk off the plane, and you'll have nothing."

"Feltham's murder was a professional hit. I'll bet the authorities have a file on you somewhere."

Silofski emerged from the direction of the flight deck and joined the conversation. "I've heard most of this, and it is damaging, Mr. Blackman."

Blackman exploded. "You have no real evidence. You can't prove anything."

Teresa Holmes seemed to be enjoying the argument. "Maybe there's more hidden evidence in his Suite."

Silofski nodded. "Good point, madam." He turned to Blackman. "I am senior captain on flight and have ultimate authority. Marcia, I authorize you to go and search Mr. Blackman's Suite." His eyes turned back to Blackman. "There have been two murders, and I am not risking another or any other incident. I am placing you in restraint."

Blackman screamed at him, "You don't have jurisdiction."

Silofski addressed the assembled passengers. "Yes. I do. The captain of airplane has total authority." He followed this statement with another. "You may also know that crimes committed on flights follow jurisdiction of country of plane's registry. Pacifico is registered in Hong Kong, so if warranted, prosecution will occur there. And Hong Kong police and prosecutors are not always nice people." He turned to Nick and Katie. "So, it was you two who ran investigation. When you know this man was killer?"

Katie spoke for her husband and herself: "Just a short time ago when Nick discovered he didn't work for the building security firm, we put two and two together."

Teresa seemed to be enjoying the exchange. "So, what happened? How come Feltham was on board, and how did Blackman get to her."

Nick nodded. "I'm not sure of everything, but here is what Katie and I have."

Teresa was excited. "Please go on."

Nick signaled to Katie, who watched Ned intently as Nick laid out the plot as they saw it. "One or more players in BioContra committed fraud, and Trisha Feltham, an IT contractor, discovered the crime. She contacted the FBI, but somehow, BioContra found out about her and decided to have her silenced before she could pass over her evidence. Feltham needed corroborative evidence and decided to travel with the BioContra people, hoping to engage one or more in conversation about her findings and record these."

Borders asked, "How do you know all this?"

Nick answered him. "From a bunch of email printouts Feltham had with her."

Borders interrupted again. "If she was an IT person, why would she have printouts of the emails?"

Katie shook her head. "I'm not sure why, but we think she assumed the internet on the plane wouldn't work."

Nick continued. "She was suspicious that BioContra might be onto her and expected she was under surveillance. She went to the gym to mislead them and then straight to the airport. Blackman followed her there and bought a last-minute ticket. Captain Silofski set up a call for me with the Booking people in Pacifico, who verified the timing of the purchase."

Katie added, "Why Blackman killed her when he did, we don't know. But it was just after she had sent an email, and Blackman could have overheard that and decided to kill her before she sent any more. It would have been smarter to wait till we were closer to Bali."

Grange nodded. "His choice of cyanide was brilliant. Smuggling the murder weapon through TSA was easy, and the likelihood of the death being classed as natural was high. He didn't expect someone like me to be on board."

Teresa continued to show her excitement. "Why did he impersonate a homicide detective?"

Katie answered. "Who better than a detective to lead the onboard investigation if there was a suspicion that it was a murder? When we found out he was not a cop, he had to change his story." She addressed Blackman. "I'll bet your client was one of the BioContra executives, but you probably don't even know who it is."

His silence and slight smirk told them that he could make the identification.

"Perhaps the CFO?"

He looked away, confirming her guess.

Everyone's eyes were on Blackman, who seemed to make up his mind. "I can give you the person who hired me, but in exchange, you must set me free when we reach Denpasar. You can advise the cops afterward, and they may catch me, but I have a chance this way, and you'll have the real villain in this plot."

Captain Silofski grunted. "I not make deals with paid assassins."

Jeff had brought a pair of flexi-cuffs and a roll of duct tape at Nick's request. Jim Borders grasped Blackman's hands, and the Passenger Service Manager slipped on the cuffs and tightened them. Blackman struggled, but Borders was strong and half-carried him to the back of Business Class, where Jeff used the duct tape to secure him to a seat.

Anthony Stamford spoke rapidly before turning to return to his Suite. "I've had enough excitement for now."

Katie asked Nick, "Do you think he was part of it?"

"I don't know, but if Blackman identifies his client, the police in the U.S. should be able to link him in if he was involved. Hey, we can't do everything for them."

As they did this, Marcia appeared back at the bar, holding up some documents. "These were in a hidden pocket in his carry-on. Passports. Three of them. Same picture, different names, different nationalities."

Chapter Twelve

There was a screech of tires as the A320 set down at Ngurah Rai International Airport in Denpasar. Nick looked out at the palm trees surrounding the landing strip, glistening in the early morning sun.

Katie called over to him. "Did you get it done?"

"Yes. I finished before I had to pack my laptop away for landing. All our notes are in a file and I have attached it to an email for the local police. I need their email address and an internet connection. I press the enter button, and we are done with the mystery.".

"Good. Now we are truly on honeymoon."

"Flying First Class on Pacifico was a treat, but a couple of murders and a near crash weren't on my agenda."

"Nor mine."

The story was not quite over. Blackman, or whatever his real name was, was formally arrested by the Indonesian police. The local detective unit grilled each passenger and crew member before releasing them to depart for their hotels. Separately, a detective inspector met with Nick and Katie. He was a thin man of about five foot eight dressed in a shiny, bright green suit. He wore a white shirt with a flamboyant lime green tie that did not quite match his suit. "Mr. and Mrs. Bunn, I apologize for keeping you here all this time, but we must gather all the facts about these murders." He flicked through a printout of Nick's email and supporting spreadsheet and nodded his approval. "This report you've prepared is excellent and has most of what we need. Great job, you two."

Nick smiled at the policeman, and Katie said, "We're happy we could help."

"Where are you staying?" he asked them.

"The Adiwana Warnakali on Nusa Penida."

"Very nice. Remote. Your notes and our discussion should be everything we need, but we may have to contact you again. How long are you staying at the Adiwana Warnakali?"

"Four nights. Then three at an Airbnb in Canggu and four more at the Visesa Ubud Resort. We fly back to the U.S. through Singapore after that."

The inspector scribbled some notes in a small leather notebook and turned his attention to their passports. "Your passports say you are Bunn and Pittlekow, but you describe yourselves as Mr. and Mrs. Bunn."

Katie smiled at him. "We are Newlyweds. Pittlekow is my maiden name, and we haven't had time to change my passport yet."

"Newlyweds? Wonderful. Congratulations. This must be your honeymoon. I trust you will have the best time in Bali. This murder business on the flight over was not a good start."

Nick laughed. "We like a little excitement now and then.

Katie added, "But now we just want some peace."

The inspector bowed his head a little. "Your sleuthing has largely solved the case, and you've made my job much easier. But I've kept you at the airport for far too long. You need to get to your hotel."

Nick sighed. "I think it's quite a way."

"It is. You must first go to Sanur Beach Harbor. Then, you take a fast boat to Penida Island." He reached for a small radio and barked some instructions into it. "I can help. I'll have a car drive you to the harbor. The traffic in Bali is terrible, so we'll use our siren. It will cut the one-hour drive to about thirty minutes."

They reached the harbor in just under thirty minutes and boarded a boat for the forty-minute trip to the island. A car from the resort met them, and fifteen minutes later, they were entering the hotel's reception area.

Nick announced. "Good morning. We have a reservation."

"Your name, sir?"

"Bunn. Mr. and Mrs. Bunn."

The End

The Wedding

The Honeymoon Mystery is a fictitious story but is based on the real-life wedding of Nick and Katie Bunn, which took place on October 26, 2024.

The Ceremony took place at St. Paul the Apostle Church, Horseshoe Bay, TX, followed by a Reception at The Retreat at Balcones Springs, Marble Falls, TX

The couple was supported by their parents Brian and Margaret Pittlekow and Harry and Jackie Bunn with a wedding party of twenty:

Jeanette Pittelkow - Maid of Honor

James Bunn - Best Man

Brinley Zheng - Bridesmaid

Ali Dastjerdi - Groomsman

Carson Hooper - Bridesmaid

HARRY F BUNN

Andrew Mavis - Groomsman

China Davis - Bridesmaid

Anthony Ridgley - Groomsman

Janelle Curtis - Bridesmaid

Caleb Ringkob - Groomsman

Julia Lane - Bridesmaid

Flynn Walker - Groomsman

Manilia Plummer - Bridesmaid

Grant Harvey - Groomsman

Talia Shalen - Bridesmaid

Grant Metersky - Groomsman

Vernisha Andrews - Bridesmaid

Nathan Ondracek - Groomsman

THE HONEYMOON MYSTERY

Willow Peterson - Bridesmaid

Scott Wo - Groomsman

About the Author

Harry Bunn is known for his spy thriller series *Purple Frog* and his adventure/romance novel Delta23, set in 2091. He also published a nonfiction book on Customer Experience strategies for B2B companies.

Harry has traveled to over fifty countries worldwide and has resided in Sydney, Australia; London, England; and Princeton, NJ. He founded an international marketing consulting firm focused on the technology sector, managed it for thirty years, and is now retired in St. Croix in the U.S. Virgin Islands, where he lives with his wife, Jackie. They have two sons, James and Nicholas.

Contact him at

harrybunnauthor@gmail.com.

The Purple Frog Books

Purple Frog: A Thriller (Book 1)

Jason Overly, a technology billionaire, funds a daring rogue operation devoted to world peace. This international team employs unorthodox methods, including hacking, blackmail, extortion, and occasionally, murder. The group has been given the name Purple Frog after a little-known frog that spends most of its time underground, out of sight, emerging only for two weeks each year. Keeping below the radar is key to Purple Frog's success, but a plot to assassinate the new president of the European Union calls for more direct action and the risk of discovery.

MetalWorks:A Thriller (Book 2)

Frederik Verwoerd is successful and rich but wants more. He desires to become a major player on the world stage and decides that his South African armament company, MetalWorks, will develop a new weapon of mass destruction, which he will sell to the highest bidder. The weapon is neither nuclear, chemical, nor biological, but can destroy an army of five thousand tanks in the field, or even a major city. To demonstrate its power, he targets a well-protected symbol of the United States and will telecast its destruction live.

It falls to Purple Frog, a private and clandestine organization, to stop him. To do so, Purple Frog must reveal its existence to the CIA. However, the Russian president has already threatened to locate and punish the organization.

Brotherhood of the Skull: A Thriller (Book 3)

Outside Washington, DC, one million armed white supremacists have assembled to march on the capital and seize power. They are led by Gideon Page, a charismatic but ruthless white supremacist, and Jonathan Greer, a televangelist. They have a symbol for their insurrection: an ancient skull previously owned by Adolf Hitler. A rogue U.S. senator, Jeffrey Kendall, has teamed up with them and expects to become the new president of the United States after the Brotherhood of the Skull overthrows the present elected government.

Law enforcement is hamstrung by legalities and political correctness, but the clandestine Purple Frog organization has no such limitations and moves to thwart this attack on American democracy.

Citadel of Yakutsk: A Thriller (Book 4)

"The Citadel is the real threat." The dying words of the CIA Chief of Station in Moscow are cryptic, but no one knows what his message means.

Yakutsk is a remote city in Siberia. It boasts the coldest weather of any city on the planet and is home to a clandestine facility in subterranean caves deep beneath the conurbation. This secret metropolis is the headquarters of Alexi Rackov, a Russian general who has developed a plan to expand Russian territory by invading eight countries and bringing eighty-eight million European citizens under Russian hegemony. While there are rumors about such a site, these only identify its name: the Citadel. Its location and mission are known only to Rackov and Dobry Petrovski, the Russian president.

In the United States, Purple Frog is a secret organization established by Jason Overly, a tech billionaire, with the mission to foster world peace. Though Purple Frog parallels the CIA and MI6, it operates outside the rules and political correctness of these intelligence organizations. It will face its greatest challenge as its small team strives to prevent the annexation of these Eastern European countries.

Flag Eight: A Thriller (Book 5)

A new president in Venezuela, Mateo Videgain, is facing a multitude of problems, including a collapsed economy. He regards the United States as a major reason for this and his main enemy, deciding on a bold plan to consolidate his place in history.

Just 520 miles to the north is the U.S. territory of St. Croix, and Videgain decides to invade and occupy the island.

All hell breaks loose as, with help from Russia, his helicopters, warships, and troops attack. When the locals fight back against his vastly superior forces, the battle is short and the Venezuelans take control.

Few countries have been ruled by seven different nations, but over the five hundred and twenty-eight years since Christopher Columbus discovered St. Croix, it has been a territory of Spain, France, the Netherlands, England, the Knights of Malta, Denmark, and most recently, the U.S. In total, seven flags have flown over the island. The Venezuelan president raises his flag over the territory—flag eight.

He has not, however, factored in that Jason Overly, who has a home on the island, is also the head of a clandestine intelligence operation called Purple Frog, which will do whatever is necessary to stop the Venezuelan president's plans.

To Venice with Love: A Thriller (Book 6)

Alan Harlan and his new wife, Jess, embark on their honeymoon to a Greek island, but they encounter an old enemy and a Saudi prince who have deployed a bioweapon on an ecologically advanced super yacht. Alan and Jess find themselves on the vessel's maiden voyage from Athens to Venice, discover the plot, and need to identify which of the passengers or crew will be responsible for triggering the device on their arrival in Venice.

Alan is head of operations for Purple Frog, a clandestine organization that mirrors the CIA and MI6 but with fewer constraints. He brings many of Purple Frog's resources into play as they battle the forces striving to destroy this romantic Italian city's population and one million visiting tourists.

Delete Code: A Thriller (Book 7)

Mike Young, a computer hacker, develops a set of malware that can delete every file and every piece of software from any computer that he targets. Initially, he sees this as an approach to extort money, but others see it as a powerful weapon of destruction. After successful demonstrations of the code's power, a major enemy of the United States develops a plan to use it to further its goal of world domination. The cybersecurity forces in government and the corporate world find themselves unable to counter the threat, so it falls to the hackers and field operations staff of Purple Frog to isolate and remove the danger.

Brisa's Grief: A Thriller (Book 8)

The head of a drug cartel, a billionaire, a spy's wife, and a killer experience grief and resolve it in different ways.

A DEA team raids the headquarters of a South American drug cartel, but things don't go as planned and the daughter of the cartel chief seeks revenge on the United States. She develops a new narcotic which she plans to release, killing several million Americans.

With political tensions running high, the U.S. governmental agencies are unable to act, and the task of preventing the disaster falls to Purple Frog, a clandestine organization devoted to world peace but without the constraints of conventional intelligence organizations.

Assault and Battery: A Thriller (Book 9)

November Swan is the third richest person in the world, but his portfolio of companies is turning sour. To tackle this threat, he decides to go "all in" acquiring a startup company that is developing next-generation, solid-state batteries for electric vehicles.

His plan requires access to rare earth components which are needed for large-scale manufacturing. These are located only in China.

Having always skirted the law and regulations, Swan pushes into more criminal acts to achieve his objectives, including a deal with China that puts the U.S. economy and its security in peril.

The Purple Frog team is tasked with stopping him.

Final Bow: A Thriller (Book 10)

In the face of an unstoppable force, the only option left is to fight back.

In Final Bow, the world hangs in the balance as an alliance of China, Russia, North Korea, and Iran develops an offensive they call "Global Strike." With the future of the Western world at stake, the clandestine spy team at Purple Frog must decide whether to use their own bold and risky plan for world peace, accepting its ethical and practical risks.

With the stakes so high, the tension builds as each move brings them closer to the ultimate showdown and the death of one of Purple Frog's leadership team becomes a final bow.

Delta23

Delta23 describes the world as it might be in the year 2091, providing the backdrop for a fast-paced science fiction adventure.

Hut Mur spends his days driving a space tractor delivering goods across the solar system. but his dull life is interrupted as the Earth faces its greatest threat of the century and he is called on to meet this unexpected challenge.

With a touch of whimsy in the footsteps of The Hitchhiker's Guide to the Galaxy, Hut Mur must embark on a journey to save the world. Combining danger, romance and a taste of adventure, this thrilling story will keep you on the edge of your seat.

Non-Fiction

Customer Experience: It's not that easy.

Customer Experience Programs for B2B Companies

Customer Experience programs are gaining momentum in small and large companies, but most have been designed for the Business-to-consumer (B2C) model. When the approaches that work for B2C are applied in the Business-to-business (B2B) world, they fail.

Based on 27 years of experience consulting to major, global B2B companies, including IBM, Hewlett-Packard, Microsoft, Dell, VMware, EMC, Samsung, AT&T, Verizon, BT, Telefonica, Honeywell, Motorola, Accenture, Nokia, Siemens, Fujitsu, and Xerox, Harry Bunn sets out practical approaches for the B2B world. This book shows how Customer Experience can be built into the culture, the strategies, and the actions of companies together with the mechanics required to "get it right". It shows how current customer satisfaction programs can be transformed into Customer Experience programs providing companies with sustainable, competitive differentiation.

THE HONEYMOON MYSTERY

Made in the USA
Monee, IL
23 September 2024

65658219R00121